Doors on the Wall

Henry lives quietly in Cambrid̵ ̵̵̵ ̵̵̵ ̵̵̵ ̵̵̵ ̵̵̵ Great Uncle
Norman but without his Mum, who has been missing for
two years. Uncle Norman thinks Henry would be happier
living with younger members of the family but Henry
wants to stay with him.

His settled life begins to change when he meets an unusual
busker at the Christmas market, who seems to know him.
The man is, unseasonably, playing his mother's favourite
folk tune, '*Scarborough Fair*' and he dresses like someone
from another century.

When Christmas Day arrives, Henry's life is turned upside
down as he finds himself suddenly pulled out of his time
and into another with no obvious way of returning. From
here he must work out a way to get home again.

He soon makes some surprising discoveries there that will
change the way he sees everything.

And he finds help from new friends, particularly a man
called Tom and a very mysterious cat named Biddy, who
seems to belong only to herself......

Doors on the Wall

By

Christa Davidson

To George, (+ Mummy
+ Davy)
with much Love

Christa
x x

With cover art by

Oliver Pengilley

For Big G for inspiration, for Glen who encouraged and helped me so much and for Annabelle and Cleone, who love books.

I hope you like my little book, I had a lot of fun writing it.

Contents

1. Biddy

2. Uncle Norman's Idea

3. The Man at the Market

4. The Cat in the Painting

5. Fifteen Hundred and Eighty

6. A Familiar Face

7. "Remember Me to One Who Lives There"

8. Plots and Plans

9. "She Once Was a True Love of Mine"

10. Rosemary for Remembrance

11. Parsley for Bitterness

12. The Invitation

13. Startling Discoveries

14. Party Preparations

15. Traces of Henry

16. Unravelling Mysteries

17. Brother Jok

18. The Day of the Party

19. Jok Goes Travelling

20. Sir Rupert's Hospitality

21. Rescue Plan

22. A Proposal

23. Disappearance Discovered

24. Remembering Home

25. Danger in the Tower

Are you going to Scarborough Fair?

Parsley, Sage, Rosemary and Thyme

Remember me to one who lives there

She once was a true love of mine. . .

Chapter 1

Biddy

H e n r y George Paterson was lost in the world of his book when he heard his name being called from the living room of the house, 16 Highcroft Ave, which he shared with his Great Uncle Norman. He just called him Uncle Norman though, the full name being rather a lot of words for everyday use.

"Henry!! Can you come downstairs for a minute please?"

Henry huffed a bit as he was reading a good bit, but he levered himself off his bed and went to the door.

"Coming Uncle Norman!" He shouted, tripping over his untied laces on the stairs but righting himself just in time. His laces were often undone and his buttons were often done up wrong too. Uncle Norman never seemed to notice.

He ran down the stairs and arrived in the sitting room where Uncle Norman was enjoying his morning cup of tea.

Henry George Paterson had bright red hair, big blue eyes and a sensitive, gentle kind of face. He had a

1

sad look in his eyes which you could pick up if you spent long enough with him and caught him in an unguarded moment. He lived alone with his Uncle Norman who was a kind and gentle man, although living alone as a bachelor for his whole life had made Uncle Norman set in his ways and sometimes a bit grumpy. When Henry was younger he had felt slightly intimidated by him but now he knew him and on the whole, he was a good person to live with. Either way he was the only family Henry George Paterson now had.

"Ah, there you are," Uncle Norman said as Henry arrived a bit breathlessly at the door of the living room, after nearly tripping on the stairs. Uncle Norman's tall, long limbed frame was leaning back in his favourite armchair. He still had his public-schoolboy's haircut, but what used to be foppishly floppy, was now thinning and wispy and had a way of standing straight upwards when caught by a breeze. This meant Norman was always smoothing it down when he was outside. Henry wished he would cut it as it was a bit embarrassing in front of his friends. He also had grey bushy eyebrows, (which looked as if they had their own independent life) and a serious manner about him. "Would you go next door for me and pick up a letter? It was sent to the wrong address. Gladys just called to let me know. There's a good lad." Henry wondered why Uncle Norman couldn't go himself but didn't argue. (The truth was Uncle Norman was also reading a book which he didn't want to leave.)

Henry had had very little to do with Gladys but he had once encountered her cutting her rosebush in the garden next door. She was very thin, quite short and slightly bent over. If you saw her from a distance you could be forgiven for thinking she was a man. She had extremely short hair and wore baggy trousers and a checked shirt to do her garden. She has been quite glamorous at one time in her life, but not these days. She also had a beautiful cat with a little pearl collar called Biddy, who had come into his garden one day and then run back into Gladys's garden. He had taken a chair to look over the hedge at the cat and lo and behold, there was Gladys busy raking leaves. When she had seen his head looking into her garden she had said, "Young man, it is extremely rude to stare into other people's gardens! Be off with you!"

He had felt a sinking feeling in his tummy and jumped off the chair feeling hurt. He hadn't meant any harm. What Henry didn't know was that Gladys had just returned from shopping at Archbury Court with a group of lads following her and calling her, "Old Man Cooper" (Cooper was her last name). She was well aware that she was not as glamorous as she had once been and she wasn't usually bothered about it, but still, it had put her in a bad mood.

That was his last meeting with Gladys and he didn't much like the idea of another one. But he was an obedient boy and so he said, "Yes ok," pulled his jacket

on, and headed out into the damp and grey of a
November day.

He stood on Gladys's doorstep with his heart
beating a little faster than normal. He wondered why
Gladys hadn't just brought the letter round herself.
What he didn't know was that Gladys loved people
calling round (when she wasn't feeling grumpy) as she
was quite lonely and usually invited them in for tea.
When Gladys opened the door, she was glad to see the
little red headed boy standing there as she was aware
that she had been very abrupt with him the last time
they had spoken and she wanted to make amends.

"Hello there!" she said.

"Hello," said Henry.

"You've come to pick up that letter for your uncle I
expect?"

"Yes."

"Come in..." said Gladys.

Henry, slightly unsure, but encouraged by her
friendliness, wiped his feet on the doormat and stepped
inside. He closed the door behind him and the outside
noise of traffic passing turned instantly into a quiet
hum.

The clock in the hall seemed to be ticking loudly
in the sudden decrease of noise. He looked closer at it.
It was a clock of a type Henry had never seen before
and he liked it. It had a round centre and sun rays made
of brass around the outside of it. There was also a

painting of a castle next to it that caught his eye. He loved castles. He looked at it for a few seconds and then followed Gladys into the kitchen where she was saying, "Would you like some Ribena and a biscuit Henry?" He didn't really want to stay long...but said, "Yes please," to be polite. He sat down at the kitchen table and looked around.

The kitchen would have been very fashionable in the 1950s when Gladys and her husband had bought the house, but now it felt like a place caught in a time warp somehow. Henry didn't recognise that the style was 1950s chic but he knew it felt old...faded. Gladys had not moved on in her tastes since that era. He sat down on the plastic kitchen chair and looked at the duck egg blue walls. He was a boy who noticed things, noticed details and colours. He was thinking about all this almost without realising, when Gladys placed a glass of Ribena before him. Its purple colour reflected onto the kitchen table in a transparent shadow as the sun shone through the glass. She offered him a custard cream which he took shyly. The clock ticked. Henry bit into his biscuit. He thought the crunching sounded loud.

"Henry, I am so sorry that I was rather cross with you the last time I saw you," she said, looking at him over her glasses which had slipped down her nose. "I wasn't in a very good mood that day, I know I can be a grumpy old woman at times...can we start again and be friends?" Gladys looked kindly at the little face with freckles and blue eyes. She noticed the quiet manner of the boy, his eyes taking in his surroundings.

"Yes, ok," said Henry. He wasn't sure he knew how to be friends with a lady that he considered to be old...but it seemed like the right thing to say - and she had kind twinkly eyes. Yes, he liked her after all. He smiled and crunched his biscuit.

"Good," said Gladys, returning his smile. "Now where's that letter for your uncle? Oh dear, I don't seem to be able to remember where I put things these days." She got up and wandered into the next room to look. Henry took a sip of blackcurrant and waited. He felt a bit awkward somehow and looked forward to going home.

Just then, there was a light clacking noise at the back door and Biddy the cat walked in. Henry stopped feeling awkward and leant down to call the cat to him. Biddy walked over to him and sat down. She looked him in the eyes and they examined each other. She looked at him with the unblinking stare of a cat and assessed him. He looked back at her. Her eyes were interested green pools and looked as though they had seen a thousand things. He felt warm inside. In that instant, they were friends. Biddy got up and curled herself around his legs purring loudly.

"Here it is!" Gladys's voice became louder as she came back to the kitchen. "I left it in the...oh wow!! You are honoured Henry. She never does that to anyone she's just met! Well, well - She really likes you!!"

"I like her too," said Henry, stroking her head. Gladys looked at the purple Ribena stain and biscuit crumbs around his lips and smiled.

"You may come around and see her...and me...whenever you like," she said.

"Thank you!" said Henry, still feeling shy but pleased. "Well I better be going now; goodbye Biddy." He reached down to give her another stroke. "Goodbye Gladys...thank you for the drink and biscuit."

Gladys handed him his coat which he put on and opened the front door.

The door closed behind him and the sound of traffic became louder again. Henry felt relieved and pleased. The whole experience had been much nicer than he had thought it would be and he had made friends with Biddy. He began to think of when he could go back and see her again. He put the letter in his pocket, opened the garden gate and walked back up the path to his own home.

* *

It had been two years since Henry's Mum had disappeared...nobody knew where she had gone but one day...she just wasn't there anymore. No letter to explain, no clothes taken...just...gone. The police were still investigating the case...well, at least, it was still open...but the general idea was that she had run away somewhere. There had been lots of talks with Henry around the time it happened...gentle talks, talks about things he didn't know all the answers to.

"Did Mummy seem unhappy before this happened?", "Did she have any new friends?" Henry hadn't known if she was happy or not...she had seemed alright to him.

Henry's father had died before he was born, and now after the Disappearing, Henry was to all intents and purposes, an orphan. Sometimes he dreamed about his Mum. His beautiful Mum with the strawberry blonde hair and she always seemed to be calling to him from quite nearby, almost as if she was in the next room. He never saw her face, but in the dream, he always got the feeling he was meant to follow her somewhere. He didn't enjoy waking up from those dreams much. Day to day he managed not to think too much about her. Her going away was a sad, sad thing he had buried deep in his heart. Usually after he had these dreams he woke up and cried that she wasn't there and they weren't real.

* *

His uncle was a scholar, a man who wrote very thick (and Henry thought boring) books about extinct animals. He had studied at Cambridge University, the town where they still lived. Henry and his mother had moved in with Uncle Norman a year before she had gone, to help him with house work and the arrangement had worked well. He gave them a place to stay and she had helped out with cooking and cleaning so he could study more.

Once she had disappeared Henry and Norman were thrown together. He really wasn't an unkind person but he was a man of study who had never married and enjoyed long hours with books. He wasn't someone who was used to having children around or who knew how to talk to them. He was a man with a strong desire to do the right thing and it seemed obvious and right that Henry should stay with him.

Uncle Norman did the best he could, trying to remember what it was like to be nine. He even found his old train set he had kept in the attic all these years for Henry to play with. Henry did like these little engines and the signals and track...but he had been brought up on computer games and they weren't of huge interest to him. Norman was sometimes impatient with his great nephew and this is what Henry interpreted as unkind. He had never had the discipline of a father and had only known his mother's love. She had told him off sometimes, of course, but he knew that she *knew* him...and liked him so it had never stung.

Uncle Norman and Henry had some connections sometimes, playing with the train set together. When Henry had gone to sleep, his great uncle would sometimes sit smoking his pipe and look into the fire muttering to himself, "Poor little fellow...what will become of him?" He was getting older and there was no one else that could take Henry in once Norman was gone...no one really except...but she was too far away...or was she? Norman would sit in thought weighing up different options and consequences and puffing smoke out of the corner of his mouth.

Chapter 2

Uncle Norman's Idea

T h e next day at breakfast, Uncle Norman opened the letter. He hadn't had time to read it the night before as he'd gone out to a lecture about the demise of the Quagga (half horse, half zebra...a species that had become extinct long ago) and had returned quite late at night. Henry had been to sleep over with his friend Jonathan and had returned in time for a late breakfast. Uncle Norman opened it with a brass paper knife he had inherited from his father. It had an eagle's head on it. "Crrrrrrrw". "This is the one I've been waiting for," he said half to himself, half to Henry and he walked thoughtfully out of the room to read it in private, running his fingers through his grey hair.

Henry went upstairs to his room and absentmindedly read some comics. He thought he might phone his friend Jonathan later to see if he wanted to come around and play video games. He thought of Gladys and Biddy. He thought about the funny clock and the picture of the castle in Gladys's hall. He remembered Biddy's beautiful white coat and her liking him and her green eyes that seemed to look into his heart somehow. Suddenly, the bedroom door squeaked open quietly and slowly, but it made him jump. He had not heard his uncle climbing the stairs.

"Henry, can I talk to you about something?" he began. "

Yes," said Henry.

His uncle came in and sat on the edge of Henry's bed. It creaked slightly as the springs gave way. The noise seemed to be very loud suddenly as there was a certain tension about Uncle Norman that made Henry feel uneasy. Norman said, "Um" and then, "Ah" and then shifted and said, "Let's go downstairs and have a drink Henry."

"Ok," said Henry. He wasn't thirsty but Uncle Norman seemed to be putting off what he wanted to say. Henry felt a sudden twist in his tummy...was something wrong?

He waited patiently while drinks were made and poured, (Norman even made himself a cup of tea) and the biscuit tin was brought out. Crunching and sipping he waited nervously to hear what his uncle wanted to say. Uncle Norman's feeling uncomfortable was making Henry feel very much the same way.

"Henry...hmmm...hmmmmmm! hmmm...hmmmm!" Uncle Norman cleared his throat twice, then pulled a white handkerchief out of his pocket and blew his nose.

"Henry...ummm...it's been two years, Henry since your mother...since she...and I have been thinking long and hard about what is best for you in the long term."

"Oh," said Henry and crunched nervously. His mouth felt dry. He felt a pang in his stomach and he didn't like it.

"Henry, I am really quite an old man you know?" (Henry wondered how many times Uncle Norman was going to say his name in this conversation.)

"I really love having you here Henry," he said. "But I can't help thinking about...well, you know, as I get older...you know...ahem...that there should be options...options, old boy so to speak...do you see what I mean?"

"Not completely," said Henry.

"Well look Henry, the fact of the matter is..." (Norman suddenly became clear and confident in his speech and manner) "...the fact of the matter is that living here indefinitely with an old man like me won't work forever. Henry, I think, in the absence of your mother, that you really need a woman to help bring you up. You're missing that maternal love all children need. And what if the worst should happen to me...?"

He looked at Henry and Henry looked at him. It seemed to Norman as though Henry's face was made up entirely of huge sad blue eyes.

"There is my goddaughter, Lisa, who is a wonderful person...she has agreed that if it became necessary you could go and live with her and her husband. They are lovely people Henry…" he said quickly, seeing the boy's face drain of colour. "I know how you must be feeling Henry but you must know, I only want the best for you."

Henry was thinking and feeling something horrid. Until this moment he had always half-thought that his Mum might come back. It was in the back of his mind. As his great uncle spoke he realised that she wasn't...that it was necessary for arrangements to be made for someone else to look after him...that he might have to leave. This was devastating.

While still absorbing this thought, Henry said quietly, "Where do they live? Will I still be able to see my friends?"

Norman cleared his throat again. "The thing is...they actually live in Canada old boy, I visited them there once, it really is a lovely place to live..."

Norman carried on talking about the lovely farmhouse they had in Ontario and how they had never had children and so wanted to...but Henry had stopped taking in what he was saying...instead his mind was filled with spiralling thoughts, 'Canada!'

"Henry...I've been wondering if you would like to go for a visit in half term to meet them. That letter was from them. They would love to meet you and see how you all get along. If you get on well and you want to, you could move over there as soon as you like. It can't be all that much fun living with an old man like me."

"What?" he said. "Leave you and this house? Have I done something wrong Uncle Norman?" His freckles stood out in sharp relief on a face that had gone quite pale. His uncle's face looked suddenly tender and concerned. "No Henry, No. It's just that...well I'm not as young as I used to be and...I want you to have a proper family to take care of you. I want you to be able to have a mum and dad again. If anything happened to me...I don't know where you would go old boy."

"No!" said the normally quiet Henry suddenly, surprising his uncle, so that he nearly knocked his teacup off the table. "No, I don't want to! I don't want to!" He ran from the room, his eyes filling with tears, emotions whirling in his mind that he couldn't find words for. Canada? What about his friends? What about this town? It was all he had ever known! He felt unwanted, and scared. What was going to happen to him?

Downstairs Norman lit a pipe and puffed anxiously out of the window. "Oh dear," he said. "That didn't go too well".

Henry ran upstairs and threw himself on the bed, crying. He didn't want to leave Cambridge. It was his home. It was where he had last been with his mum and dad. He cried because he had realised Mum was gone...really gone. He cried until he reached that stage when you feel a bit tired and worn out and then lay with his head on the damp pillow wondering what to do next. He knew uncle Norman had said, "What did he think...?" about going to Canada, which probably meant he didn't absolutely have to go. It almost meant, though, that staying here wasn't really what his Uncle wanted him to do and that thought made him feel sad and scared all at once.

He got off the soggy pillow and played listlessly with his Star Wars Lego for a while. Then he wondered if he could think of a reason to go next door again to see Biddy. He peeped out of his window and saw that Gladys was outside doing some gardening again. "I'll see if she wants any help weeding," he said to himself. He knew a bit about weeds from helping his uncle out at times.

He got up and got his coat quietly as he didn't want to talk to his uncle at that moment. He saw Uncle Norman puffing on his pipe and looking out of the window as the morning sun streamed through the window. He looked worried and was frowning slightly. His head was towards the window and he didn't see Henry. Henry wrote a quick note, *'Gone next door to see the cat and Gladys'* and let himself out.

He spent a quiet and pleasant afternoon helping Gladys in the garden and playing with Biddy, who seemed very pleased to see him again and kept rubbing around his legs. Stroking her soft fur made him feel comforted. He felt the sadness of earlier slipping to the back of his mind.

When he was going home Gladys left him to get his coat while she went to get something from upstairs. He took it from the hook by the door and then turned around as Biddy was purring loudly and meowing as if she was trying to tell him something.

"What is it?" said Henry crouching down to stroke her and then straightening up again. He came face to face with the picture he had noticed before of a castle. It overlooked the sea and the sun was sparkling off the water. Henry looked at the bottom of the picture and saw the words *'Scarborough Castle'* on a small brass plate. Henry liked castles and was looking interestedly at it, when all of a sudden something very odd started to happen.

Slightly at first… and then stronger and stronger, he noticed a tingling feeling in his hands and feet. He had a funny rushing feeling in his tummy and then the room began to swirl around. All this happened very suddenly while he was still looking at the picture; a matter of seconds. Worrying that he was getting sick, he sat down suddenly on the stairs and held his head. The rushing swirling feeling stopped nearly straight away although he still felt tingles in his hands and feet for a bit. Rather scared, he shouted up the stairs, "I'm going now...not feeling well." He went home, hoping he wasn't getting the flu. He'd had it last winter and remembered feeling very dizzy with it...but the feeling didn't come back. Once he got home he felt quite OK again. 'Strange,' thought Henry George Paterson and went to eat his tea.

Uncle Norman sat opposite Henry at the supper table and lent over to him and put his hand on his arm. "Henry," he said. "I do want you to be here with me very much. Please don't think I don't. I just want what's best for you...if you don't want to go to Canada at half term you don't have to." He cleared his throat, "I'm...ah...I'm very fond of you my boy."

Henry looked up and smiled at his uncle, who was never usually so affectionate. "Thank you. I love you too," he said, feeling much better. "Shall we play with the train set after tea?"

"Yes let's," said Uncle Norman.

They both pushed it all to the back of their minds, the future and all that it may hold to be contemplated another day. They occupied themselves in the meantime with boiled eggs, Marmite dippy soldiers, Battenberg cake and toy trains and they were quite satisfied.

Chapter 3

The Man at the Market

T h e trees had shed their leaves like last year's fashion and waved goodbye to them as they floated off in the November winds. They now stood bare, their whole shape exposed. The oak tree outside Henry and Uncle Norman's house shook his branches and wished his leaves back.

Beneath him, Uncle Norman and Henry shut the front door of number 16 Highcroft Ave and walked out of the driveway. They were both dressed in hats, scarves and gloves. They looked like woolly parcels wrapped up against the cold December wind.

Christmas was coming! Uncle Norman and Henry were taking the bus into town to see the lights switched on and do a little shopping. The shops were open till eight each Thursday until Christmas. Uncle Norman had a car but was very pleased with his free senior citizen's bus pass and used it as much as possible. Anyway, at this time of year trying to find a parking spot would have been nigh well impossible.

The bus turned a corner and through the window they could see the warm lights of the windows of the Cambridge colleges and shops and shoppers clutching bags and hurrying by. Henry felt a little rush of excitement and squeezed Uncle Norman's hand. Norman squeezed his hand back. He too felt a boyish excitement in the festive atmosphere.

They stood together by Parkers Piece and shouted "3-2-1...switch on!!" with everybody else, their breath coming out like smoky steam and floating away. The white snowflake-shaped lights shone festively above their heads and made a glowing road in the air pointing towards the town centre. They made their way to 'The Copper Kettle' and ordered hot chocolate and mince pies. It was crowded but they found a seat fairly quickly. Out of the window loomed the stately turrets of Kings College highlighted by street lamps and Christmas lights. Henry munched and looked at them. He liked the shapes. He felt cosy and happy. Uncle Norman remembered doing his research studies on Zoology there and was reminiscing a little about his student days. Henry listened with interest. Norman had got up to some antics as a student, including keeping watch as an intrepid fellow student had climbed up Kings College Chapel to the top of one of its turrets and put an umbrella there which had been found the next day. Henry looked at his serious uncle, finding this hard to believe and laughed out loud.

Following this, Henry asked if he could go window shopping by himself. Uncle Norman hesitated then agreed that he could for half an hour, saying, "Take care not to chat to any strangers." Uncle Norman then headed for a second-hand bookshop to find a little Christmas present for himself. Henry headed off down Kings Parade towards the market. He was heading for the toy shop. He felt, being nearly eleven that he was maybe too old for toy shops but if no one was looking he still went and checked out the latest action figures. He was also on the hunt for a present for Uncle Norman. He was trying to think of something to bring him more up to date, he wasn't sure what.

He walked towards the market place and, then, quite suddenly, he heard a sound at once strange and familiar...

Its plaintive sound rose like a bird, soaring above the Christmas crowds. The activity on the streets seemed to fade away. He felt a tingle of anticipation and recognition go through his body in a rush like electricity. "What was that!?" he said under his breath, wondering at his body's reaction to the sound. It sounded almost as though it was calling him somewhere. As if it were asking a question.

He knew the tune being played well.

'Are you going to Scarborough Fair? Parsley sage, rosemary and thyme. Remember me to one who lived there... She once was a true love of mine.'

21

It was the song his Mum had most loved and he felt that old familiar ache in his heart. She had loved the Simon and Garfunkel version and had it on cd. He quite liked it himself although he wouldn't have admitted that to his friends. He also thought it sounded strange in contrast to all the carols playing and being piped out of the shops around him. Then he realised something even stranger. It should have been drowned out by all the noise around him, but it was as if everything else stopped and Henry could hear only that. Utterly intrigued, he followed the sound. He turned around the corner and into the market square and there...he was.

He stood calmly, almost serenely, with his eyes closed, playing his penny whistle. A faded red jacket and old looking brown trousers covered a tall and broad body. His hair was mostly grey but in the light of the shop window in front of which he was standing there glinted a hint of the red hair the man had once had. He had large hands which looked huge next to the thin whistle he was playing. He almost caressed it as he played, treating it gently as though it were made of finest porcelain.

He looked out of place and time, playing his sad and plaintive sounding song. His playing was so simple and yet he was attracting a small crowd because he played so beautifully and maybe because of how he was dressed as well. As Henry went closer to listen to him, he saw he had a white cat sitting near him. He bent down to stroke it...why...it couldn't be!

"Biddy?" he said questioningly.

The cat that looked just like Biddy purred and rubbed around his legs.

But it couldn't be her, could it? She was much too far from home.

Henry looked up at the old man. Somehow, he looked as though he belonged in another time. Henry had been to see a Shakespeare play with his uncle last year. He didn't understand much of it but Uncle Norman had thought it would be good for him to go. He thought the musician's clothes looked like the ones the actors had worn.

The old man looked at him and smiled and then did a double-take. He stopped playing. A few people in the crowd looked back at Henry. The man looked at Henry rather intently, which made him uncomfortable.

'What's his problem?' thought Henry. He began to back away. The other children and parents closed the gap. When he looked back the man was still looking after him. He kicked a coke can and felt a bit uneasy. He wove his way through the crowds and made his way to the toy shop. He lost himself looking at the latest action figure and planned a Christmas list.

Chapter 4

The Cat in the Painting

C h r i s t m a s day finally arrived with all the anticipation and excitement that it brings to the heart of a young boy, no matter what difficulties he faces the rest of the time. Uncle Norman had brought home a beautiful Christmas tree from the market one day in the back of the car and had squeezed it in through the front door smelling of pine and damp. He too loved Christmas, although in a quieter sort of way. Henry and Norman had decorated the tree together one evening to the sound of carols. There were old baubles and lots of decorations Henry had made at school over the years, as well as some chocolate ornaments. The countdown had begun and then, after a trip to hear Kings College Choir on Christmas Eve and a rather fitful sleep, Henry awoke to the sight of an overstuffed rugby sock (Uncle Norman's old sock from college days), bulging with goodies and tied at the top with a piece of tinsel and a balloon. Following bacon sandwiches for breakfast, then after opening stockings and a Christmas Day service in town, they were back at home and dinner was being prepared. They had picked up Norman's old professor friend Humphrey on the way home to share Christmas with them.

Uncle Norman was quite a good cook for an old bachelor and the delicious smell of sizzling roast turkey was soon filling the house. Henry and Humphrey had helped by peeling the potatoes.

Henry had been put in charge of feeding Biddy whilst Gladys was visiting her niece in London for the season. So, just before dinner, he slipped out into the beginnings of a light snow flurry and let himself in through her front door.

The big old oak tree saw all this, as he saw everything and sighed, 'Merry Christmas Henry.' But to Henry it just sounded like leaves rustling in the wind.

Gladys's door squeaked open and Henry let himself into an empty house. He was immediately aware of the sounds and smells of Gladys's home...things he didn't usually notice when she was there. The sunshine clock ticked loudly in the quiet. He called for Biddy but she was nowhere to be seen.

Thinking of his stocking presents and feeling pleased and happy, he went into the kitchen and pulled out a tin of cat food, scraping it into the bowl. He thought how much he would have liked to have seen Biddy. He also thought about his dinner cooking next door. He sat down at Gladys's kitchen table for a few moments and enjoyed the feeling of being in someone else's house when they are not there. Without Gladys, the house felt like an empty shell waiting for her return.

Gladys's little nod to Christmas was a tiny tree in the living room with the lights all turned off, of course, and a few cards here and there. He was glad he had a big twinkling tree to go back to.

He thought suddenly of his Mum...and felt the desolate empty feeling begin to rise in his heart. So, he pushed the thoughts back down and made his way to the door of the house. He glanced at the sunshine clock. It was 1.45pm. With thoughts of dinner on his mind he turned away...and then turned back with a question. His eye had caught the picture of the castle that he had seen last time. Had he imagined it...or was there a white cat right in the very corner of the frame? He didn't remember seeing that before. He looked again, staring intently at the cat and looking at the paint-work. Henry enjoying painting too. He was pretty sure a new art book lay under the Christmas tree at home for him to open after dinner. Suddenly he heard the cat-flap open and shut. He turned around to see Biddy run into the kitchen and towards the food bowl. He went to stroke her and when she had finished eating she came and rubbed around his legs just as she always did.

"Well Biddikins," he said (he would never had said this with anyone else around), "I'm going now. Merry Christmas!" He put his coat back on and made for the door. He opened it and a few delicate snowflakes, like tiny white feathers floated slowly and silently in through the front door and settled on the mat. He hoped there would be more snow and was very excited.

26

Suddenly, Biddy started meowing again rather intensely by the stairs. "What is it Bid?" said Henry, going back for one more stroke. He straightened up smiling, and...then...his tummy flipped over in surprise. The white cat had gone from the painting! He stared and stared, wondering if he had imagined it. He stared at where the cat had been as if expecting it to reappear. Suddenly he became aware again of the same tingling feeling he had experienced before at Gladys's house. He stood still, staring at the picture and then just as quickly as before, that rushing feeling in his tummy began. Then the room began to whirl around.

This time Henry knew that he wasn't ill and that something was happening that was...'Out Of the Ordinary.' He shouted out loudly in surprise and fear.

The room continued to swirl around until it was no longer recognisable as a room but just a whirl of colour, like being inside a multi-coloured tornado. The brass tones of the sunshine clock; the warm yellow of Gladys's wallpaper; the dark wood of the stairs, the white of Biddy's fur were all blurring together. It seemed this would go on forever. But then, all at once the colours began to change and turn to stone grey, dark red and bright orangey-yellow.

The whirling began to slow and the fizzy tingling feeling began to subside and Henry's stomach stopped churning. All this time his feet had been firmly planted on the floor and he hadn't moved. But the room had.

Now the whirling became slower and slower until it stopped. Henry's heart thumped in his chest and his mouth went dry with fear. For he was no longer standing in Gladys's hallway. The colours of whirling grey, red and yellow turned out to be the dark cold stone of a wall, a red tapestry wall hanging and the yellow flickering light of candles. Henry George Paterson was not in Highcroft Ave any more with a delicious Christmas dinner and an art book waiting next door. He was standing in what looked like a round room in a castle. Before he had time to even imagine what possibly could have happened he realized that he was not alone in the room. He saw the back of an armchair with a small hand visible resting on a large shaggy dog. He saw that he was in a bedroom and quickly slid underneath the bed away from sight. Out of the corner of his eye he saw what looked like a white cat's tail disappearing through the window. In two seconds, alerted by Henry's movement, the dog jumped up and was nosing around under the bed.

"What is it Rufford?" said a voice. Footsteps followed the dog, then a face appeared. A very pale chubby face with sad questioning eyes. "OH! Who are you?" it demanded.

* *

Meanwhile, Norman turned down the carols on the radio and looked at his watch. "Where is Henry?" he wondered aloud to Humphrey.

He knew that Henry could be a daydreamer at times and lose track of what he was supposed to be doing. He hoped he wasn't doing anything he shouldn't in Gladys's house. He didn't think he would be...but...what was taking him so long? "Can you stir the gravy please Humphrey? I'm going to see where he has got to," he said.

"Of course, Norman. I'll keep the home fires burning!" said Humphrey

Mildly irritated with his great nephew, Norman put on his coat and shoes and left the house. He went up Gladys's pathway and knocked on her door. He waited.

He knocked again. "Henry!" he called and then again though the letter box. Silence. "Henry... Henry!!"

He tried the door but it was locked and Henry had taken the only key. Had Henry gone into the garden? He went back to his own house and into the garden. The breeze blew his wispy grey hair until it stood completely upright. He looked over the fence and there was no one there. The bare trees and rose bushes looked back at him as if to say...'Nothing to see here!'

Brushing down his hair, Norman walked back into the house. He wondered if Henry was in the loo at Gladys's house. With a slight frown, he decided to give it five more minutes and then think again. He felt some old familiar emotions arising from a time two years ago, when someone else had gone out for a walk and never come back...but he pushed the feelings away.

He went back into the kitchen, turned off all the pots and pans on the stove and took the turkey out of the oven. He went into the dining room where the table was all laid up for Christmas dinner and took out three crackers which he placed by his, Humphrey and Henry's places at the table. His tummy rumbled. He then went onto the living room where Humphrey was reading the Radio Times and lit his pipe. "No sign of him!" he said

"Oh dear, really?" said Humphrey. "I wonder what's taking him so long!"

Norman poked the fire until it roared and placed another log on it. He sat back and puffed - once... twice...where in the world was Henry?

Chapter 5

Fifteen Hundred and Eighty

H e n r y felt relieved to find that the owner of the voice was a boy about his age. He slid out from under the bed and the two boys stood and looked each other up and down. The boy before him was quite chubby, a little shorter that Henry. He had blue eyes. He was dressed in clothes Henry had never seen before except in films. He was wearing something Henry didn't know the name of, but was called a doublet and around the neck it had what was called a ruff. Henry thought it looked very uncomfortable. He would have giggled if he hadn't been so scared. He also thought it was strange that the boy was wearing what looked like tights to him.

The boy looked at Henry and stared at his 21st century clothes in disbelief. He came forward to touch the logo on Henry's T-shirt in amazement. He did not seem alarmed at all, just rather curious. Henry brushed him away. He was still very on edge and bewildered.

(Now it is important to say that in reality, Ben didn't talk quite like he does as written here...but if it was written here you wouldn't understand most of what was said. As for Henry, something about being there

31

and getting there in such a magical way meant that he could understand everything perfectly well and they could understand him too. He was actually speaking the way that people used to speak then although he didn't know it. He just opened his mouth and all the right words came out somehow. This is something he never really thought about until much later on.)

"Who are you, I said?" he repeated and blinked hard. "And where did you come from? For the door didn't open and you just appeared!"

Henry looked at him. He thought he might as well tell the truth as not. He was a truthful boy anyway so he wouldn't have told a very convincing lie.

"I'm Henry...and I think I just came through that picture on your wall. Although I'm not sure..." he said trailing off and looking confused. Then suddenly he had an idea. "Are you in a historical re-enactment?" he said looking again at the boy's clothes and remembering going to one such thing with Uncle Norman once.

"What is that?" said the boy. "No indeed...I am Benjamin and I live here."

"I need to get home!" said a frightened Henry. "My uncle has made Christmas dinner and he's waiting for me!"

Visions of presents and turkey floated through his mind...it all seemed unreal and far away...what was happening to him?

"Christmas was eight months ago," said the boy whose name was Benjamin, "...and what do you mean you came through that picture...are you mad?"

"No!" said Henry. "I've got to try to get home if I can." He ran desperately back to the picture again and waited. Nothing happened. He shut his eyes and tried to make the spinning feeling happen. It didn't. He counted to ten, still with his eyes shut and then opened one to see. He saw the picture and heard the fire crackle behind him. Nothing had changed.

"You are mad," said the boy. "But...I don't really mind...do you want to stay with me? I don't know many boys my age...you see...my father..."

Just then, there was a sound of feet approaching down the corridor and Henry looked in horror at Benjamin. "Quick!" said the boy. "Hide under the bed!"

Henry dived underneath and found himself face to face with a spider...they weren't any better than the ones at home. He looked at It and It looked at him and twitched an eye.

The door was knocked on and then opened after Benjamin said, "Come in!" and in came a young woman. Henry could only see her feet and kept as still and quiet as he could.

"Your supper, Master Benjamin!" said a friendly voice.

"Thank you Thomasina."

"Do you want supper by the fire, Sir?"

"Yes please."

"How are you tonight?" she said.

"Fine thank you," said Benjamin looking a little anxiously in the direction of the bed.

"Did you enjoy your lessons today with Mr. Baggott?"

"Yes, not too bad," said Benjamin.

"Well...I can see you're not really in the mood for chatting tonight," said Thomasina. "So I'll leave you to your meal. See you tomorrow."

"No, I'm not really...thank you...see you tomorrow," said Benjamin smiling at her.

Usually Benjamin would have enjoyed chatting to the friendly maid but tonight he was anxious to resume conversation with his new friend.

Henry noticed dimly that she had called Benjamin "Sir" and that he must be important. He looked at the door which was open and thought about making a run for it. But Thomasina was too quick for him. She was at the door before he could blink and saying, "Goodnight!"

As the door swung shut, Henry realised that running without knowing who was outside the door, how to get out, or where he was going had probably been a bad idea. And besides, his tummy was rumbling at the smell of the food she brought in. His head was swimming with questions, but most pressing was the need to go home and after that, the rumble of his tummy.

Benjamin said, "Do you want some supper?" He said it slightly reluctantly as he enjoyed his food and wasn't used to sharing anything.

"Um...yes please," said Henry shyly. He hoped it was alright but he knew he had to eat. "What is it?" he asked.

"Looks like Pullet broth," said the boy sliding off the bed.

"Oh," said Henry.

He went by the fire with Benjamin and shared his meal. It was chicken with some kind of squashy lumps in sauce and it was quite good although he had never tasted anything much like it before. If he had known the squashy lumps were actually prunes he wouldn't have eaten them.

Once his hunger was dying down he started to feel calmer. This was real, he knew that now. Somehow...he could hardly believe it...but somehow, he had travelled through space and time and now was here...where was here?

Benjamin's voice broke into his thoughts. "I don't really know where you're from and everything but it is good to have someone my age to talk to."

Henry said, "Why don't you have any other children to talk to?"

"My father, who is lord of this castle, doesn't let me go out. He says he wants to keep me safe as his only heir. I am his only son and my mother died."

"Oh!" said Henry. He realised that they had something in common at least. "I haven't got a Mum either," he said, but not really wanting to go into more detail right then.

"Did she die too...?"

"Well...sort of..." said Henry then quickly moved on...

"Why does your father think that it's not safe for you to go out?"

"He says the village is full of peasants who are dangerous and wild and would take my life if they saw me. So, I never get to go out...only sometimes at night he takes me out in his carriage under cover where no one can see me."

Henry though this sounded very strange. He also didn't like the idea of wild and dangerous peasants. He took a mouthful of chicken. He wondered what sort of place he had arrived at.

"I'm sorry about that," said Henry.

"Yes," said the boy... "Thank you. It is lonely but at least I have my dog."

Henry had forgotten about the dog and looked to the fire where the dog was lying sleeping. He looked like an enormous rug. His ear twitched. Henry didn't think he looked like the world's best conversationalist.

"What's his name?" said Henry. He felt very sorry for Benjamin, in the midst of feeling so confused himself.

"Rufford," said Benjamin. Both of Rufford's ears twitched and his tail wagged slightly.

"I like him," said Henry.

There was a short silence as they sat looking at each other. The fire crackled. Outside a breeze was getting up.

"Can I call you Ben instead of Benjamin please?" said Henry thinking of his friend from school with same name.

"'Why?" said Benjamin "That's my name."

"It's easier," said Henry. "Shorter, you know."

"Well...very well..." said Ben, not wanting to lose his only new friend.

"Can I call you Hen?"

"No!" said Henry then he realised Ben was laughing a bit and he laughed too.

Then Henry suddenly had a thought...something that had been one of the questions whizzing around in his brain but he hadn't asked...he hardly dared...but he found himself saying... "Ben...what year is it?" He noticed that his heart was beating slightly faster as he waited for the answer.

"What do you mean?" said Ben. "It's 1580, of course!"

"What?" said Henry. He heard the words but he couldn't absorb them. They went around and around in his brain. He felt sick and dizzy. Somehow the picture had taken him back in time then.

"Why did you ask that?" ventured Ben.

"Because I come from 2011!!" said Henry before he thought it through.

"2011?" said Ben... "I think you really are mad. ...oh dear." He was wondering if this was one of the wild and dangerous peasants his father told him about. He wasn't sure if he should let him stay here. Should he call a guard??

Yet Henry didn't seem mad...he seemed nice... and yet...maybe that meant he was more dangerous than ever. After thinking about it he decided to wait and see how things progressed. If Henry became threatening in any way, he would call a guard. He was very lonely, enough to even take this risk. He looked at Henry's shoes...they were made of a material he had never seen before in his life. He looked at his strange clothing...such bright colours and strange images on them. He had never seen anything like that...not even the bright colours his father wore were anything like these...and around Henry's wrist was his plastic watch. Ben had never seen anything like that before...could he be telling the truth? After all how did he get into his room...when the door was locked to his outer chambers, without anyone seeing? Could his story actually be true? He decided to give him the benefit of the doubt. He decided to talk more to him. He chose the subject they had touched upon earlier.

"So, your mother died too?" he said

"Well actually," said Henry "...she just disappeared."

"What do you mean?" said Ben

"She went out one day and...never came back." Henry muttered. He didn't much like talking about this with a stranger.

"Are there peasants where you live too?" said Ben, wondering if Henry's mother should have stayed in her house like he had to.

"No," said Henry. "At least I don't think so," he added (as he wasn't too sure what peasants were).

"My mother died when I was very small of the pox," said Ben.

Henry wasn't sure what the pox was...he wondered if it was the same as chicken pox...he had had that when he was younger. He was surprised to hear it could lead to death. Ben however was talking about a disease called smallpox.

"I'm sorry," said Henry. "Can you remember her?"

"No," said Ben. "She died quite soon after I was born."

"Oh no," said Henry sadly.

Then he said, "My Mum disappeared when I was six so I remember lots of things." He wondered why he was talking like this and realized he had never met anyone his age before who knew what it was like to not have a mum. A couple of tears rolled down his cheek which he brushed quickly away. That aching feeling was back in his heart.

Ben thought that Henry didn't really seem mad after all. But that meant only one thing...that he was telling the truth!! He really did come through the picture...and from another time.

At the same time, Henry was thinking about his Mum's disappearing...had she been visiting Gladys...had she gone through the picture too?

They both looked at the picture at the same time... Henry said, "I wonder if ..." and Ben followed with, "Do you think your Mum could have...?"

"Gone through the picture too?" said Henry

"Oh, my goodness!!!!" Hope filled his heart and surged through his body.

"My Mum might be here...she might be alive! I've got to look for her!" He scrambled to his feet, his heart racing. "Maybe that's why I'm here!"

Ben didn't want him to leave and felt sad but knew he could be right. It was worth considering. He thought of his own mother and what he would do. He knew he had to help Henry.

"Why don't you sleep here tonight?" he said. "It's dark outside. In the morning, we can think what to do. You're right. You have to see if you can find her."

Henry didn't know how he could sleep but he knew Ben was right. "Alright," he said.

They sat by the fire together.

"Henry," said Ben. "Are you really from 2011?"

"Yes I am," said Henry.

"What is it like?"

"Oh...I dunno...well, we have cars...and computers...you don't have those..."

40

"Stop..." said Ben. "What were those words you just said?"

"Cars and computers," said Henry. "Cars are sort of...carriages without horses and computers are like...are like..." He tried to think of how to describe them. "They're machines..."

"What are machines?" said Ben.

"Oh dear," said Henry. "Well...they are special...um...instruments that you can communicate with and play games on and..."

"That sounds fun!" said Ben.

"Yes, it is. I play on mine all the time," said Henry.

"Maybe you could bring me one through the picture sometime," said Ben. "If you ever go home and come back again that is", he added.

"I could," said Henry "...but you don't have electricity...or the internet...so..."

"What are those things?" said Ben.

"Oh...it's too difficult to explain because we have so many things you don't know about. I don't know where to begin."

"I would like to visit your time," said Ben. "You said there were no peasants there either...I would be able to walk about freely." He gazed off into space and tried to imagine it.

"Well," said Henry. "There may be no peasants but there are other things."

"Anyway..." he said. "If I can't get back I don't know how you would be able to visit. But maybe one day..."

They chatted in this way until it got late and they began to feel rather tired. Ben gave him a blanket from his bed. It was made of fur and he curled up with it beside Rufford in the warmth of the fire. Ben got into his own bed. The blanket Ben had lent him was thick and warm, although a little rough. His head was swimming... His mother could be here too!! Despite his thoughts and the strangeness of the day he found himself drifting off to sleep. Outside he could hear the sound of waves...wow...they must be by the sea! He hadn't noticed that until just now. Henry loved the sea. The fire crackled and the dog stirred. The orange glow shone on them both as they dreamed. What would the morning bring?

Chapter 6

A Familiar Face

D a w n came and a tomato red sun rose on 16th century England. Henry stretched and vaguely wondered why his duvet felt so scratchy. He opened one sleepy eye and it all came flooding back in a rush. He was here...here!! In a...castle...in another century, with a dog and a boy called Benjamin. He felt a bit light headed again and lay down, tummy fluttering. Then he remembered more...his mother might be here too! He jumped up...the sleepy feeling left instantly as a surge of adrenalin went through him and he went and woke Ben. Ben after rubbing his eyes and going through the same remembering thing as Henry, suggested that Henry have a good breakfast before heading off. He wasn't afraid of Henry being hurt by the peasants as he thought that Henry wasn't important and they wouldn't bother him. He told Henry this, which made him slightly annoyed but he didn't say. He was a little worried himself by the idea of going out but the thought of finding his mother made up for it. He wondered what Uncle Norman was thinking...but he knew he couldn't do anything about that.

After breakfast brought in again by Thomasina, Henry and Ben began chatting more about how exactly he could get out. Ben had tried once but it was no good. He didn't really want to leave anyway as he really was too frightened. Henry privately thought he was a bit of a wimp but didn't say so to his face. He looked out of the castle window (which didn't have any glass) and wanted to see if there was any way he could get out that way. He thought, if he put his foot carefully in the uneven stones he could possibly climb down. The ironic thing was that he wasn't all that far from the ground...it was amazing how fear could keep someone trapped when escape was so easy. Sure, it might take a bit of courage and possibly the use of some sheets knotted together...but he really thought he could.

"Can I use some of your bed sheets and tie them together?" he said.

Ben balked at this as he knew they were very expensive linen...but he was caught up in the adventure with Henry and wanted to help. It was the most fun he had had for...well...ever!! He had a tutor coming to teach him fairly soon so he suggested they get on with it or they would be caught. He found some quite scruffy clothes for Henry to wear...obviously, he couldn't go wandering around 16th century England in what he had arrived in. They were old clothes belonging to Ben but of course they still looked fairly expensive, so Ben and Henry ripped off the ruff around the neck and made a couple of rips in other places as well. "Why not rub some dirt on them as well when you reach the ground?" Ben said. Henry did wish he could have worn his nice 21st century clothes instead of this get-up but he quite saw the logic. He had his others wrapped up in a bundle of cloth.

They then turned their attention to planning the escape. They tied one end around a bed post (the bed was oak and very solid) and faced each other. Ben suddenly reached forward and gave Henry a hug. He hung onto him.

"Please come back again," he said, so quietly Henry nearly didn't hear him. He really was very lonely and sometimes very frightened. Henry felt a bit awkward and sort of patted Ben on the shoulder. He felt very sorry for him and said he would if he could...at any rate he could promise to try, and then gingerly he began letting himself out of the window with Ben helping. "Goodbye Ben!" he said. "Thank you!!"

He and Ben had checked to see if any guards were on duty and it appeared to be all clear. The fact is they hardly guarded that side of the castle. Sir Rupert, the lord of the castle just never thought of Ben trying to escape. He had woven a net of fear around the young boy's mind and it held him fast.

Henry remembered his abseiling lessons from going away to an adventure park with his school and did his best to use the techniques he'd learnt there to get to the bottom. It actually was a little further then he had thought and he found he had to let go and jump quite a way, but it was a soft landing. He got up again a little breathless but fine.

Ben popped his head out of the window and quickly said, "Goodbye!" and, "Come back again...please..." Then he wiped his eyes quickly and then his head went back in through the window and he was gone.

Henry stood suddenly aware that he was all alone in another time and place with no idea what he was doing or where he was to go but he determined to go on.

He took a deep breath. It was fresh and clean. He could hear seagulls and the sound of waves. He could smell the salt in the air. He felt invigorated and very awake and alive. He felt a delicious thrill go through his body as he realised that he was in another time...actually in another time! He had often wondered what this would be like and now it was happening! He wondered if his being there would change history...he didn't want to think too much about that. "I expect I'm meant to be here and so it will all be fine," he said to himself hopefully.

He looked around. He was standing at the top of a hill covered in trees which spread to the bottom of the hill and onwards. At the bottom of the hill he could see a small collection of houses where the trees began to clear and it was these towards which he decided to make his way. He took a deep breath and started to descend the hill. It was quite steep but he made his way, stumbling here and there. He tried not to think about wolves. He had read they roamed England in earlier times but he didn't know when this had actually been referring to. He kept going down holding on to trees here and there until he had nearly reached the bottom when he tripped on an old oak root and went rolling to the bottom of the hill, crying out as he fell.

He lay there for a minute, shocked, with adrenaline coursing through his body. He got his breath back and groaned as he realised he had bashed his knee on the way down. He became aware then of voices and noises. Animals bleating and mooing, people calling out. He knew he was near to the little town he had seen. He got up, limping slightly and made his way towards the sounds

He came out of the woods and into the town. He turned a corner and immediately his senses were assaulted with a variety of sights, sounds and smells. The smell of meat cooking and freshly baked bread. Other smells were not so nice and they made him pull a face and hold his nose. He paused to take it all in. It was a busy scene with people walking here and there...some carrying vegetables and some with livestock. He soon realized he had come upon a market day. This was good as he could be less recognisable as a stranger in their midst.

He looked around and was fascinated by the scene before him, taking in everything around him. There were fruit stalls and livestock being sold. There were people selling fleeces and others woven fabric. It struck him that the colours of the clothes were less bright than the ones in the 21st century and he was glad he had changed out of his. He would have really stuck out like a sore thumb. He wove his way around the edge of the market and managed not to get eye contact with anyone. He wondered if these people were the wild and dangerous peasants Ben had talked of. Some shouted loudly but it was nothing he hadn't heard in the market place in Cambridge. He began to wonder more if Ben's father wasn't rather a tyrant, who had been lying to his son and keeping him locked up... 'But why?' thought Henry.

"Well then young master...!" Someone suddenly called out and he looked up quickly... "Buy my fine apples...ten for a penny!"

"No thank you," said Henry. He hoped he didn't have to say too much because he might say something wrong and give himself away. He looked at the lady selling the apples and noticed she had some teeth missing at the front. Otherwise she looked quite friendly and pleasant although she looked sharply at him as he darted away from her. He stopped to look at a few more stalls, all the time being careful to avoid conversation.

He was wondering what to do next when he heard a familiar tune floating on the air...

'Are you going to Scarborough fair? Parsley, Sage, Rosemary and Thyme...remember me to one who lives there ...she once was a true love of mine.'

Interested, Henry followed the sound. He turned into the middle of the market where he saw a young man singing along to the tune an older man was playing on what looked like a penny whistle. Henry only saw the back of him. By his feet was a white cat. Henry stared as he looked at the old man and took in his white beard and hair. He looked familiar. He looked very much like the man he had met at the market at Christmas back in...well, his own time. But he couldn't be the same man. Strange that he was playing the same tune though.

He wished he could have something to eat. He went and looked, from a little distance, at the bread being sold. He wondered if it tasted ok. It certainly smelled good. The man behind the stall looked at him, looking at the bread and seemed to be trying to decide something. Then, quickly, he beckoned him over and slipped a bread roll into his hand. "There you are young master," he said. "You look hungry - but don't be telling anyone else about this or they'll all be wanting one! On your way now." Henry took it and mumbled his thanks. He tasted it a bit nervously, but he needn't have worried. The bread was good and tasted much nicer than the sliced wholemeal from the supermarket that Uncle Norman bought every Thursday. More like the homemade bread Mum used to make.

He went back and watched the musician again...this time from a different side of the fair, where he could see the man's face. He sat down, took another mouthful bread then looked up.

He froze mid-chew. He felt his heart start to beat faster. He was looking straight into the face of the very same man he had met in Cambridge. The man's eyes slightly widened as he looked back but he said nothing, just kept playing. Henry was confused and bewildered, yet thinking fast. So, this man could travel through time too? Was he from the 21st century or this one? How did he know who Henry was...he remembered him calling out to him at the Christmas market...? He felt afraid and walked quickly away trying to stay calm...what did this all mean? He was turning the corner when suddenly a white cat curled around the side of the tent and then around his legs.

"Is she bothering you?" said a voice affectionately. Henry looked up. The old man was there. He hadn't noticed the song finishing. His heart leapt into his mouth... "No"

"She shouldn't do," said the man. "I think you've probably met her before." Henry looked down and recognised the cat, "Biddy???" he said incredulously. The cat purred and did another circuit around his legs.

"How did...did she come here when I did??" He remembered the end of a cat's tail disappearing though the castle window in Ben's room.

The man didn't reply to that but said, "We've met before too, of course...you remember?"

Henry nodded, "At the market in Cambridge."

"That's right," said the man. "That was me...I'm Tom...pleased to meet you." He did a little half bow.

"I'm Henry," said Henry

Tom gave him a funny look, as though a puzzle piece had fallen into place and gave out a relieved sigh.

They looked at one another for a minute. Tom looked as though he was struggling with some emotions.

"Henry," said Tom... "do you think you can trust me?"

Henry looked into his eyes...they were different colours...one blue, one green. He kept looking and felt peace go right through his body suddenly, "I think so," he said, surprising himself.

"Good," said the man. "Now let's go and have a chat somewhere we won't be heard."

Henry knew all about never going anywhere with someone you don't know.

"No..." said Henry. "I won't come with you, I'm sorry. I do trust you, I think...but..."

"Yes, yes, quite right...quite right indeed," said Tom stroking his beard and looking thoughtful.

Biddy purred and rubbed around Henry's legs.

"I have some very important things to talk to you about...shall we talk about them right here?" he said, sitting down on the grass next to Henry.

"Ok," said Henry. There were lots of people about and so he agreed.

He sat down on the grass, stroked Biddy and waited for Tom to start speaking.

* *

Uncle Norman had waited for Henry for another hour before thinking about calling the police. He had gone around to Gladys's house again and banged on the door till his knuckles hurt. He thought of him lying, hurt inside, unable to get to the door, or possibly unconscious. He was a rational man and told himself not to be dramatic. Henry might have gone to one of his friend's houses. Unlikely, but not beyond the realms of possibility. His friend Jonathan lived just the next street over and maybe, for some reason, he had gone there. He rang him first and then all of Henry's friends that he could think of. "I'm sorry to call on Christmas Day, but..." he tried to downplay the urgency he felt.

"Oh no, he's just popped out..."

"Been a bit longer than expected and I wondered if he might be with you...sorry to disturb..."

Norman sat for a brief minute in his armchair to collect his thoughts.

The presents lay untouched, glimmering in the Christmas tree lights, seeming out of place with what was happening. He had offered lunch to Humphrey and he had agreed as he was rather hungry. So, while he got stuck into the sage and onion stuffing, Norman worried and smoked his pipe. Yes, he finally decided, he had exhausted all the options. Hardly believing this could be happening again, he reached for the phone with a familiar sick empty feeling in his stomach and this time he dialled 999, "Police please."

Chapter 7

"Remember Me to One Who Lives There..."

T o m spoke in a low voice as he didn't want others to hear what he had to say. "Now then..." said Tom, "I'm sure you are wondering what all this is about aren't you?"

"Well, yes, a bit..." said Henry with huge under-exaggeration

"Do you have any ideas about it yourself?"

Henry looked up sharply. Biddy looked around at him and her tail twitched very slightly. Henry paused. How much could he say, was he willing to share? He decided not to and just shrugged his shoulders a little bit. "Not...really," he said.

"Henry... I'm not quite sure - but you look very much like someone I know - so much so. When I saw you at the market in Cambridge your face took me by surprise. Now that you're here as well, I'm more sure,"

Henry's heart skipped a beat, "Who do I look like he said?" quietly, his heart thundering. Could it be...?

"A rather beautiful friend of mine called Rosie," said Tom looking hard at Henry.

Henry's heart did a somersault and he couldn't speak at first...his throat was dry. Then... "I...I think she might be my mum..." He felt like he wanted to laugh and cry all at the same time.

Tom lent close to him, "I think so too," he said quietly.

Henry felt like a firework had gone off inside his head. As his hopes and the facts became one and the same Henry began to cry and he could see tears in the old man's eyes too.

"Henry, there are some things I must tell you about her which will be difficult for you to cope with. She doesn't remember you or her life in your time. You mustn't be surprised when she doesn't know you. It will be hard for you. She has forgotten. But maybe, in time, she will begin to remember."

"Why has she forgotten?" cried Henry, his heart feeling empty and sad. "I haven't forgotten her and I'm here."

"I'm not quite sure," said Tom. "But it seems that over time, when people travel back and forth as you do (and trust me I haven't met too many), you seem to have forgetfulness as a protection or the grief would be too much."

"Did she remember me when she first came?" Henry asked, crying as he spoke.

'Oh yes," said Tom. "At first. It was hard for her...very...but I looked after her. Took her in, protected

her from harm...and gradually she seemed to forget. But
now..." he said, his eyes brightening. "You're here
Henry and that might make all the difference!! But I
want to say that I don't want you to tell her who you
are straight away."

"So, is she stuck here?" said Henry

"Maybe," said the old man. "Unless she can go
back with you through the way you came. That's what
I'm hoping."

Suddenly Henry became excited, "Where is she?"
he cried. "I know she will remember me, of course she
will!"

"Well...she will soon be…" said the old man. But
before he finished his sentence a dog ran up to them,
followed by a woman carrying a bundle of clothes. She
was dressed in 16th century clothes and her head was
covered with a headscarf, but Henry would have known
her anywhere. His heart seemed to go into his mouth
and skipped a beat...it was his Mum.

Chapter 8

Plots and Plans

S i r Rupert Deverous was in his castle overlooking the surrounding countryside and thinking hard. He thought about how much he wanted a son and heir. At this time in history much as in others it was very important to a nobleman to be able to leave their castle and land to a son. The truth was, you see, that Ben was not actually Rupert's son after all. He was his nephew. His sister had died giving birth to him and his father was already dead. Rupert had spread a story about that the child had died too. He had taken the child to his castle and raised him in secret until such time that Rupert would marry and have his own son. He had adopted him legally but he planned to do away with the boy should this ever happen. But he kept him as his son and heir in case marriage never happened for him. Ben was kept a secret from everyone except three people - his maid Thomasina, his tutor Mr. Baggott and one guard. These three people had been sworn to secrecy and were paid a lot of money to keep silent. Sir Rupert knew that Ben's life was terrible, stolen from him. And yet his own needs and desires were more important. He was a clever and cunning man, able to give the impression of being kind and charming...most of his servants thought this to be true and yet, he had this secret he kept close to his chest. He hated himself for it but wanted his own way more.

Ben, meanwhile, sat with his tutor in his school room and tried to concentrate on his Latin lesson. He had been very restless since he had met Henry and longed to see him again. He often sat and thought of him, especially during Latin lessons with Mr. Bartholomew Baggott. Mr. Baggott was short and rotund, with a beard and round spectacles. He was a good man but a very dry teacher and Ben didn't like Latin. He sat and repeated after Mr. Baggott, "Do, das, dat, damus, datis, dant" (conjugated version of 'give').He heard the words and knew his Latin pretty well because there was very little else for him to do except learn. He always did his homework having very few distractions. However, his mind was far away.

Mr. Baggott looked at the pale face of this young boy for whom he felt so sorry and wondered again why he was hardly allowed to leave the castle. He hadn't been told much about it. There was some explanation that the boy was ill and couldn't leave on health grounds. He knew the boy believed it to be another reason which Mr. Baggott knew he would start to question as he grew...he had serious concerns about the boy's welfare ...but the lord, Rupert, was very careful in choosing his employees and Mr. Baggott had been chosen well. He was discreet...kept his opinions to himself and was too grateful to have employment to ask any questions. At least this is how he had felt in the beginning...now, he wasn't so sure. He hadn't been made aware of the situation fully before he had accepted the post. What was happening with this boy? How long could he keep silent...? He decided to try to talk to Thomasina, Ben's maid and see what she thought about it all.

Rupert Deverous was sitting and plotting. He knew he had to find a wife - it was so important to him that his estate went to a son and heir of his own, not just the son of his dead brother. 'Then I could mysteriously do away with that brat of my brothers,' he thought.

He planned to have a party to which he would invite all the people he knew, including the villagers. It would be disguised as the act of a 'Bountiful Lord' but it would be 'A Looking For a Wife Party' really. "There must be someone amongst the women who will do," he said to himself out loud. "It would help if she was pretty," he added. Then he remembered that the Scarborough fair was coming up and decided to make it part of the celebrations so as to not draw so much attention to himself. He also thought that it wouldn't do his popularity much harm either. He started there and then to make preparations.

Chapter 9

"She Once Was a True Love of Mine..."

T h e r e she was with the sun behind her...with red hair like Henry's, although a lighter colour, more like a strawberry blonde. Her green blue eyes stood out in contrast to her hair. She was beautiful, as she had always been…But to Henry she was just his Mum….if 'just' can ever be the right word. She stood and looked at Henry. She looked surprised to see him...but smiled warmly all the same. "Hello there!" she said and looked at Tom, with a question in her eyes. He looked very familiar to her...who was he? She knew she sometimes forgot things...maybe he was a lad from the village...

Her voice! So familiar and yet…Henry longed to run to her, his heart was hammering and his eyes filled with tears. He started shaking and Tom gently put his hand on the boy's arm.

"This is Henry," he said. "A friend I made at the market."

He then turned aside and said quietly to Henry "Would you like to stay with us Henry?"

Now that Henry had seen his Mum, the answer was easy. "Yes please!" he said. He felt as though he had been given a cold drink on a hot day...or that a blurry picture on a TV screen suddenly came into focus...the warm, relieved feeling of suddenly making some sense of being somewhere unfamiliar and unsure...of finding his place of belonging within the whole strange scenario.

"He doesn't have anywhere to stay tonight so he'll be staying with us Rosie."

"Oh!" said his Mum, smiling at Henry. Then taking Tom's arm she spoke quietly to him, but Henry could just hear what she was saying, "Are you sure Tom? Things aren't good at the moment...we don't have a lot to spare for the two of us, let alone another, with a young boy's appetite, I expect."

Tom said, "There's always enough Rosie...somehow there's always enough. When we take in those in need there's always enough. Don't you worry." Tom considered reminding her of when he took her in but thought better of it. He knew she probably didn't fully remember how she got there.

Henry felt sad that his own mother didn't want him to stay. He didn't know what to do. He felt a physical pain under his ribcage. However, his mum soon softened and smiled at him... "You're right Tom. And what a handsome lad he is!" she exclaimed. Forgetting her misgivings, she went to Henry and sat next to him on the grass. "Hello Henry," she said. "I'm Rosie."

"I know!" Henry wanted to shout and then throw his arms around her. 'I mustn't give the game away,' he said to himself. However, he managed to squeak out "How do you do Rosie?" A tear made its way out of his eye and down his cheek...

"Why are you crying?" asked Rosie leaning down so that her eyes were level with his. "What's wrong?"

"I...I miss my Mum..." Henry whispered, to his own surprise.

"Where is she?" said Rosie.

"I...I don't know," said Henry, which in a way was true. He didn't know where his Mum had gone, the one who loved and knew him. There was a pause as Tom looked keenly at him and stroked his beard and then back at Rosie...her eyes filled with tears too, though she wasn't sure why and she gathered him into her arms and held him close.

Then the tears broke free for earnest and he sobbed as he held his mother close for the first time in six years. He sobbed for the times he'd wanted her and missed her and she hadn't been there...he sobbed because she was here now but she couldn't remember him. He felt his heart would break.

Rosie felt confused but holding the young boy, she felt a strange emotion she didn't recognise...a connection somehow... a recognition...and she pulled Henry from her and looked at his face...searching it, taking in every detail.

"Why you look just like..."

"Who?" said Henry. "Who do I look like?"

"Oh, someone from a dream I keep having," said Rosie. She felt somehow that this meant something...but being a down-to-earth sort of person she shrugged it off as a coincidence, patted his shoulder and disentangled herself from the hug and gathered her bundle of clothes together and stood up, brushing off her skirt.

"Let's go home," she said. They walked toward the woods and went into the shelter of the trees.

Tom, Rosie, Henry, their dog and Biddy walked through what seemed like many trees...although the wood was not deep they were going horizontally through it.

In time, the trees became less thick and they came into a small clearing where there was an old cottage, with smoke rising out of the chimney. It looked like so many cottages in woods in stories he had read. He had always longed to go into them and now he felt like he was in a fairy tale of his very own. As far as he could see it wasn't made of gingerbread so that was good anyway. That story didn't turn out too well.

He still felt peaceful and trusting of Tom. Mum and Biddy being there helped too. Tom opened the wooden door (which squeaked) and they all went into the house.

Henry hung back for a minute in the doorway, taking it all in. It smelt of past fires and wood, a rich smoky smell. As he walked further in, he could smell the fragrance of dried herbs hanging up near the fire place. Mum had dried herbs back in their old life and hung them up in the kitchen. He had forgotten….

Tom asked, "Are you hungry?" breaking into his thoughts. He nodded…travelling through time had given him quite an appetite. Tom and Rosie started gathering the ingredients for a stew. They grew vegetables near the cottage and Henry helped his Mum dig up and chop carrots, onions and potatoes. Tom had hunted a rabbit earlier in the day which he was preparing to go into the pot. (Henry didn't enjoy watching that bit much.) Soon the whole house smelt wonderful. The fire was lit and the wood smelt aromatic and heady.

They sat down together at a wooden table and Tom brought out three wooden bowls which he filled with stew and cut them each a thick slice of freshly cooked bread.

Henry, Tom and Rosie tucked in together. "Mmmmm hungry work, playing that whistle," he joked, and winked at Henry.

The day went past. Rosie sat by the window, in the sun, and worked her way through a pile of sewing. Henry sat with her for a good long time while Tom was busy outside. He stared at her when she looked down. He looked at her hands to see…was it there? Yes - there was a small scar on her third finger on the inside where he remembered she had her cut herself on a tin of tomato soup. And there was that freckle on her neck that nearly looked like a star.

Rosie chatted to him a little bit but was always cagey because she couldn't remember very much and felt uneasy when people asked her questions. She did, of course know that she lived here with Tom and worked for a tailor in the village so she talked about that a little, never guessing that Henry had to be just as guarded. But then as they were both reserved and not wanting the other to delve deeply, it was ok. Henry felt safe and happy to be near her, but also uneasy and sad since she couldn't remember him. It wasn't exactly the wonderful reunion it should have been.

After supper, once the day was done, Rosie showed Henry to a place where he could sleep...a little bed up in the attic made by Tom himself with the softest duvet filled with goose down (Rosie told him she had sewed it herself).

"Good night Henry," Rosie said and gave him a little kiss on the cheek and laid her hand on his head for a short moment, before going out and shutting the door so that it wasn't quite closed but open a crack...how did she know to do that? It was just what Henry had always asked her to do growing up at home.

Henry lay back on the bed in the dark of 16th century England and felt slightly scared in the dark. Everything was different, even the sounds of night...no cars in the distance or going up and down outside. His feelings of unease lessened though as Biddy curled around the door and came in to join Henry. She jumped up on the bed and purring, walked in circles on the duvet trying to find the best place to sleep. When she found it, she lay down and put her head on her paws and shut her eyes. Henry found in her the great comfort that animals can be when we feel sad. He reached down to stroke her fur. She purred like a little motor engine at the end of his bed.

For the second night in a row the events of the day went around and round in his head...his head spun with thoughts and images from the day. He'd found his Mum...but she couldn't remember who he was...and they were both staying in the home of the Christmas Market Musician...how crazy! He decided he couldn't make any sense of it in his head so he tried to relax. One thing was clear - there seemed to be a bigger force at work in his life which seemed to be orchestrating all these things together. He hoped it was a good force and after one last bewildered glance at a slumbering Biddy, he too fell asleep.

Chapter 10

Rosemary for Remembrance

A l t h o u g h Rosie had brushed it off when she first met Henry she knew deep down that it had to be significant that this beautiful little boy with the huge blue eyes and red hair was someone that she dreamt of often. She couldn't remember much else of the dream but she knew he had been in it. She wondered what it meant. "Maybe I dreamt of him because he was meant to come to us and I was seeing into the future," she said to herself. She had heard of those kind of dreams...foretelling dreams. She thought about all these things, usually as she was falling asleep and when her 'common-sense' thinking was not so operative.

She was very aware of gaps in her memory. Of missing pieces in the puzzle. She was frustrated that she couldn't remember anything about her life before living with Tom who was a kind of father figure to her and a good friend. She was concerned about it and sometimes mentioned it to him. He didn't seem to be worried and always reassured her, "I know you Rosie...I've known you all my life"

"But where are my parents? If you've known me all that time you must know them too. Are they dead?"

"I knew your dear mother," he would say and then distract her by telling her stories of her mother.

"Why can't I remember her?" Rosie would say

Sometimes Rosie would have dreams with people she didn't know and places she didn't remember visiting. And of course, the one enduring dream with a red headed boy in it.

Tom had thought of telling her the truth...but something always gave him a check inside...it would be too disturbing...too traumatic. No, the best thing would be for her to go back to Cambridge and let the adult memories that she had there come back to her. She had only been away for two years and maybe it would be alright over time. Of course, she would remember Scarborough 1578 at first. The complications of time travelling. It could be quite distressing, especially when relationships were involved.

"Not worth it," he would say to himself.

"People think they know what they want but..." He thought of his brother Jok who had always talked of wishing he could time travel when he was a boy.

Tom knew he would be happy, if only he could be sure that Rosie got home and her life returned to normal ...as much as it ever would. Then he could come and see her and Henry. Somehow, he could become a part of their lives. It wasn't perfect, but it was the best solution.

Rosie could remember some things about life. She knew she loved sewing. She knew she always had. She knew some things from growing up in the 21st century that she realised others didn't...things about science and travel for example. She didn't know how she knew them and it distressed her. She mixed as little as she could with others but Tom knew and tried to protect her as best he could. Else she might have been tried as a witch.

People in the village mostly bought his story...that he had found her wandering and had taken her in. He told them she had some memory problems and they accepted that Tom had was taking care of her. He was respected by the community and everyone knew he had lost his own daughter when she was very young,

"Taken at the fair," people said to one another.

"You have to keep a tight hold on your lil' uns at the fair," "God alone knows where she is now!"

Some people had thought at first that Tom had found a young wife.

Yes, there was a good deal of talk about them when minds and tongues were idle. Some of them whispered to one another that it might even be his own daughter, who had wandered home although she didn't know her home.

Another would say, "What terrible things happened to her to make her lose her memory?" and so on and so on. She was generally regarded as someone who had some memory problems and who came from no one knew where. But as she was accepted by the village as the girl who worked at the tailors and who therefore had a place in the community she didn't get too much trouble.

Chapter 11

Parsley for Bitterness...

H e n r y was woken by Biddy purring and padding around on the duvet...he stretched...and got out of bed. He hadn't slept in his clothes, Tom had given him a night shirt to wear that was far too big for him. He slipped his clothes on and went downstairs.

Tom was stirring something on the stove when Henry made an appearance.

"Hello," said Tom.

"Hello," said Henry and then before he could stop himself, "Where's my mum?"

Tom told Henry that Rosie had already left to start work in the tailor's house in the village where she helped part time. Henry remembered how much Mum used to love to sew when he was young. She had made most of his clothes.

"What are we going to do today Tom?" said Henry.

"Well now," said Tom. "Come and have some breakfast ...do you like porridge?"

"It's ok," said Henry who wasn't a huge fan. Tom poured some in a bowl and pointed out the cream and sugar lying on the table. Henry tasted it, poured on some cream and then then added sugar. The sugar went bluey brown under the layer of cream. Henry decided he did like this porridge...it wasn't like the microwave oats his uncle had bought at times.

"I brought that sugar back from your time Henry!" Tom said chuckling

"There's no way in this world I could afford to buy it in this time. It's only for the rich."

Henry stared at the pot of sugar on the table...something he took for granted having at home.

Uncle Norman! Henry suddenly thought of him properly for the first time in two days...he must be very worried about him! He knew he couldn't do anything about that but it made him feel a bit upset.

"Are you worrying about home?" said Tom.

Henry looked up quickly in amazement, "How did you..."

"Just had a feeling...Henry let me assure you I will do everything I can to help you get back as soon as possible...I need you to tell me how you got here...which picture did you come through?"

"I came in through a picture in the castle," said Tom. "I arrived in the room of a boy my age...Ben"

"A boy your age?" said Tom. "One of the servant boys?"

"No," said Henry. "The son of the lord of the castle."

"But he hasn't got a son," Tom said.

"Yes, he has! He lives there but he never goes out, well only at night with his father. He has been told that there are wild people around here that are too dangerous for him to meet with and he seems to believe him."

"And you don't, I take it," said Tom

"No, I don't," said Henry. (He thought he would have met them by now if they were real.) "I reckon his Dad is a nasty piece of work, don't you Tom?"

"Well, it does seem unusual," said Tom. "But then I don't know all the facts." He was very curious though and wondered how he could find out anymore. Sir Rupert had a good reputation with people around here...and yet...somehow Tom had never quite trusted him.

"Anyway, it's not going to be easy to get back in there Henry," said Tom. "But there will be a way...has to be or you wouldn't be here..."

"Now I know that the people at the castle have their mending done by the tailor where Rosie works and maybe there's a way in there."

"Let me think...I'll ask Rosie if they've had any jobs from the castle this week and we'll see what we can do. It's one thing getting Rosie to the castle and quite another getting you and her into the boy's chambers where the picture is ...this is not going to be easy..."

"Let's go and visit Rosie at work. Give you a chance to look around the village. If anyone asks who you are I shall say you are the son of a friend of mine who is visiting...well it's quite true isn't it?" He laughed. Henry did too.

They set off back into the village they had been in the day before. "It's good you're here at this time of year Henry," Tom exclaimed. "It's going to be the fair soon. You'll enjoy that...quite an occasion."

"What fair?" said Henry.

"Scarborough Fair," said Tom. "People come from miles around for that, and from overseas too. Just think...you'll be able to go and attend a fair that hasn't happened there since the 1700s in your time!"

"Wow!" said Henry as he took this in. "Is that where the song you sing comes from?"

"Oh yes," said Tom. "It actually is quite a modern tune at this time and I always play it a lot as the fair approaches. It sets the atmosphere and gets people looking forward to it."

"What is it about?" asked Henry

"It about a lost love," said Tom and Henry thought he saw sadness in the old man's eyes. It passed through and went as quickly as it came.

"Look Henry we're nearly there."

They passed the houses and shops in the village. Henry looked with interest at the buildings around him. They looked very like some streets in Cambridge that he knew in the 21st century...except there wasn't a McDonald's or a WHSmith's or any other familiar places in sight. People nodded at Tom with respect and the odd person said, "Tom…" but with caution as if they were unsure of him or what he was about. Tom said to Henry quietly, as if he knew what he was thinking. "I keep myself to myself mostly…I find that's best."

They came to a small shop with the word 'Valcar's Tailor' written on a sign outside. They went in though the small doorway and stepped down into a shop with various clothes hanging in the window and a little man behind a counter who was busy measuring cloth. The shop smelt of cloth and slightly of damp too which made Henry sneeze. There was also another customer in there who caught Henry's eye straight away. He wasn't sure he liked him very much…he couldn't say why. He had dark hair and eyes and a moustache. He said, "Tom," and nodded curtly. Was it Henry's imagination, or did his eyes slightly narrow? He was sure he saw something dark flicker behind his eyes. He looked slightly familiar but Henry couldn't put his finger on it.…

"Hello Jok," said Tom, looking steadily at him. Then he turned to the shop keeper. "Hello Robert, is Rosie in?" Tom said.

"Yeess," said the man, "I don't really like her work disturbed, but go in for a minute"

He waved them around the back of the counter where there was a door into a little room. Going through with Henry following they found Rosie sitting working her way through a pile of sewing. There was a musty smell of other people's clothes. It was like the smell of charity shops but worse.

"Hello Tom, hello Henry!" she said. "How nice to see you at work...what brings you here?"

"You forgot your lunch...we brought it to you," said Tom.

Rosie looked confused... "No, I brought it with me," she said...and looked down into her bag... "Well I'll be!!" she said. "I didn't...Tom I could have sworn I brought it!! Well thank you...how strange." She accepted the bread and cheese that Tom handed her. Henry didn't remember them bringing it or talking about lunch at all. What Henry didn't know is that Rosie did forget things fairly often and this wasn't the first time Tom had had to bring her lunch to her. Henry was confused. He thought they were there to talk about the castle. But he didn't say anything about it. He was going to but at that moment Tom squeezed his hand and he didn't.

They chatted for a couple of minutes and turned to leave.

"See you at home Rosie!" Tom said. They went back through the shop...Jok was nowhere to be seen...and back out into the street.

"Why?" said Henry. "Tell you later," said Tom... "Let's go home for lunch...and after that I've got logs I need help chopping if you don't mind?"

"Ok," said Henry, trying to sound tough...he'd never chopped a log in his life. They walked in silence for some time, until Henry said, "Why didn't you ask Rosie about the castle?"

"We weren't alone...it wasn't safe to talk," said Tom.

"Do you mean the shop keeper?"

"No," said Tom. "The other man, Jok. He is not to be trusted."

"Why not?"

"He and I had a disagreement long ago," said Tom. "I was willing to forgive and forget, but he is not. He tolerates me, but these is no love lost. Once, long ago we both loved a girl, the same girl...but she was in love with me. She and I got married ... and he never got over it. Jok is my own brother, Henry."

* *

Rupert Deverous had never married. He wanted to very much as he wanted a son and heir. He had his late brother's son in the tower just in case he should never manage to procreate but his real desire was to have a son of his own. The boy thought he was his father. His mother had died in childbirth and Rupert had travelled to take the child under the pretext of wanting to care for him, but really, he was an insurance policy...a backup plan. It was unthinkable not to have someone to whom to pass down all he owned...if it was his own son, all the better. Marriage had so far alluded him. It was too much effort to go scouting around the country. He decided to investigate the possibilities. He would hold a party in the castle and see if he couldn't find himself a wife from amongst the local women.

Chapter 12

The Invitation

I t was about a week later and Henry and Tom were back at the market. Tom was playing his flute again and collecting money. Biddy was nearby. There was hustle and bustle everywhere. Henry loved exploring the stalls in the market and asked if he might go and look around. "Sure," said Tom... "Can you buy some bread please? "

He gave him a coin and Henry went off exploring, taking in all the sights, sounds and smells. It made him feel like he was at a historical re-enactment from his own time. Mum used to like those and often took him to them. 'Only this is REAL,' thought Henry and a delicious feeling of excitement and a little fear went through him, 'It's really REAL!!'

After he had looked for a while he went to the bread stall again. He was just thanking the trader for the loaf when a servant rode into the middle of the market on a horse and nailed a notice to a tree.

"Hear ye all!!" he said. "Rupert Devourous Lord of Scarborough castle is holding a Summer Party during the annual fair. All invited. It will be held in two weeks' time in the evening commencing at six of the clock."

He turned the horse around and rode off. The market was set to chattering straight away. "All invited?" He heard one lady say. "Most strange!" said someone else. The air was buzzing with excitement...not many had been inside the castle walls.

Tom was stroking his beard and muttering, "How unusual…" to himself. However, he quickly realised this could be the perfect way to get in the castle with Rosie and Henry.

"Henry!" he said. "We must go to that party with Rosie."

"Oh yes!" said Henry. "There might be a way we can get into Ben's room. It will be hard though."

"You're right," said Tom. 'And I can't help wondering,' he thought to himself, 'If there may be more to this party than meets the eye.'

Henry's friend Jonathan was at home in Cambridge in 2011 playing in the back garden when his mum appeared at the back door. "Jonathan Jones! I asked you half an hour go to tidy your room!" she said. "What are you still doing in the garden?"

"Sorry Mum" said Jonathan and went quickly in the house. He didn't want to have TV privileges taken away like last week. He went up the stairs two at a time, his new skill while his Mum watched, smiling. He was a goodhearted boy but sometimes he went into a daydream. She shook her head and walked back to her computer where she was writing a book. She had already written a book that had been a bestseller and she had a deadline for a new one.

Jonathan went into his bedroom and assessed the mess. Where to begin? He picked up some of his toys from the floor a bit half-heartedly and shoved them under his bed. As he did so his eye fell on a picture of him and his friend Henry on his birthday last year. He sat down suddenly. It was such a shock...what had happened to Henry...where was he?

Jonathan had never lost anyone in his life before and he was taking this hard. He wasn't even Henry's best friend but he really liked him and they often played computer games together.

Wasn't it funny that Henry's Mum has disappeared in the same way and now him?

Jonathan felt sad...he felt like many others whose friends or families have disappeared somehow...that they might come back anytime...and they might not. It's difficult to get on with your life. This was making Jonathan more day-dreamy than ever. He sighed and got back to tidying up his room.

Chapter 13

Startling Discoveries

"**A** r e you going to Scarborough fair...parsley, sage, rosemary and thyme...remember me to one who lives there...she once was a true love of mine..."

Tom was singing under his breath as he worked outside with Henry. Henry felt himself getting stronger and stronger with all the chopping of wood that he was doing. He felt pleased with himself as he felt his muscles getting stronger. He wished he could show some of his friends back home how strong he was getting. "I bet I could win an arm wrestle with Jonathan now," he thought gleefully. He hoped he'd get the chance to try before too long.

Then he asked Tom, "What does that song mean? I mean I know it's about the fair but what about the parsley, sage, rosemary and thyme bit?"

"Well," said Tom. "They say that Parsley is comforting or for removing bitterness, Sage is for strength needed, Rosemary, to help remember love, and Thyme for courage. Whether it is true or not, I can't say, but that is the common belief."

"Oh," said Henry...thinking that he might need all of those to get home to his time again.

"Come and sit by me Henry," said Tom. They both sat down together on the newly chopped pile of wood. They felt tired but invigorated by the activity.

"Henry, I have something to tell you." He looked down at the ground then into Henry's eyes as Henry turned to face him.

"What is it?" said Henry thinking how comfortable he felt with Tom, like he'd known him all his life.

"Do you remember when I told you I was once married?" said Tom

Henry nodded, hoping this wasn't going to one of those boring grownup stories.

"Well, I married the most beautiful girl in the world...her name was Beatrice. Her name means 'voyager through life'," said Tom. "Which is more like you, me and Rosie really. You see you and me...and Rosie...we are able to travel through time and space through pictures and other doorways. I was the only person I knew who could do it...until Rosie...and I didn't even know that until...and of course Biddy is...well, let me tell you the whole story."

Henry found a comfortable place on the ground, leant back against the wood pile and bit into some bread Tom had given him.

"I loved Beatrice...so did Jok, my brother, as I told you before. But she fell in love with me and he has never really got over it. I mean the anger and jealousy. I sometimes think he would do me harm if he could," said Tom. "I don't mean he would plan to physically harm me...but he would like to do me wrong in some way. But he is still my brother. Beatrice my love...died when she was giving birth to our daughter. Our darling was born and her mother slipped away just after. She got to hold her one time...she had the time to say, 'I want you to call her Rose.'"

Tom looked at Henry. Henry didn't blink. "We had discussed other names before...Elinor for a girl and William for a boy...but when she saw her she said 'Rose.' and I couldn't bear to change it. It was her dying wish. She was a Rose, sometimes Rosie, ever after." He looked at Henry again...no change. "Henry," said Tom pleadingly, gently, "Rose is my daughter...your mother...and so...I am...your grandfather."

Chapter 14

Party Preparations

A s the town of Scarborough was getting ready for the fair and the arrival of many visitors from far and wide, so the castle was preparing for the party. Sir Rupert himself was not overly involved in the preparations, but had chosen one of the senior servants to do it all. He has been redefined as party organiser, owing to the fact that he was known for his administrative skills. He took to this like a duck to water and was loving ordering all the other servants around. "No don't put that there!", "I want WHITE roses!!", "RED drapes!!" He was also overseeing the court jester, who had also managed to get some of his friends, who were performing fire breathing and juggling at the fair, to come and perform at the party in the evening.

Rupert walked languidly through the preparations and looked absentmindedly at the red velvet drapes. He rubbed them between his fingers. 'I hope Gyles is not spending too much,' he thought. But he did not want to get involved so he headed for the door, meaning to keep an eye on him if it got out of hand. He saw Gyles in the distance, manically waving his hands around to the cook and he thought, 'Give someone a little power and it goes straight to their head!' But he didn't care, as long as the job got done. "I hope it's worth it," he said to himself quietly. "After all most of the guests are just village folk." He quickly slipped away as Gyles had spotted him and was rushing towards him. Rupert pretended he hadn't seen him and slipped through a door to make his escape.

Upstairs in the tower Ben could smell all the wonderful food that was being cooked and said to his dog, "Wonder what's for lunch Rufford old boy. Smells good." He looked sadly out of the window and thought of his friend Henry. Where was he? Had he found his mother...would he ever come back?

Chapter 15

Traces of Henry

U n c l e Norman was at home. He had spent the morning with the police going over old ground. Just after Henry had disappeared, they had broken into Gladys house and obviously not found Henry. They had searched all the surrounding area; put posters all around Cambridge; been on the local and national news with Uncle Norman and an old school photo of Henry and just about everything else they could think of. One paper had even run a campaign to find Henry. Of course, Norman himself had been questioned heavily, but he had an alibi in Humphrey so they had made no charges. However, there was still some suspicion toward him. Norman felt worn out...worn thin. His eyes had dark circles underneath them.

Now he was back in Highcroft Avenue and Gladys had popped round to make lunch for him. She often did little practical things like this to help him now. She was turning to leave when Norman said, "Won't you stay Gladys?" And so she did.

They chatted about this and that. They deliberately didn't speak much of Henry. They talked about gardening and books. Gladys had also been to Cambridge University as a girl and loved to discuss things with Norman. She hadn't discovered this until Henry disappeared. For Norman, it was a relief not to be always thinking about Henry. She poured herself a cup of tea. "Do you know Norman," she said. "I haven't seen Biddy again for a while. Have you seen her?"

"No, not recently," said Norman looking at her over his spectacles. He wasn't a huge fan of cats but he quite liked Biddy. He always gave her a quick rub under the chin when she came into his garden before he shooed her away. "I shouldn't worry, she comes and goes, doesn't she?" he said.

"She certainly does!" remarked Gladys with a rather weary sigh.

Now Biddy was one mysterious cat. She often disappeared but also came back just at the right time. She was often with Henry and Tom these days but also appeared back in Cambridge 2011 now and again to eat the better quality food that Gladys offered. It was just enough to stop Gladys getting suspicious. Tom didn't know. And as for the matter about to whom she belonged...well that was a mystery too. But I rather suspect that Biddy thought she belonged to herself, as most cats do.

Later that afternoon Norman was in his garden, looking at the snowdrops which were starting to pop up everywhere and going over the morning events in his mind again...when he suddenly felt a soft brush over the back of his legs and a gentle meow. "Well hello Biddy!" he said in a friendlier way than he usually did. "Where did you spring from? Gladys will be glad to see you!" and he bent down to stroke her. Just as he tickled her under the chin, he noticed that she had around her neck an unusual pendant. 'Hmm, Gladys must have put her name and address on her...don't blame her,' he thought to himself.

He felt it with mild interest and his fingers found a cold ceramic shape. He looked closer and saw the letter H, with a cobalt blue glaze. He recognised it at once and his hair stood on end on his arms as he did. It was the pendant Henry had begged for on their holiday to Cornwall last year. He loved it and wore it most of the time when he wasn't at school. Indeed, as Norman had suspected it was secured around Biddy's neck with a piece of leather cord. (Norman didn't really approve of boys wearing necklaces, but Henry had bought it with his own allowance.)

"Biddy!" he said. "Is this Henry's? Is he alive? Where is he?"

He slipped it off her neck, looked at it intently and straightened up, confused. What did this mean?

As he held it he suddenly felt sure of something. Henry was alive and was trying to let him know. He felt peaceful. Biddy did another circuit around his legs purring, trying to tell him all was well. Norman was right. Henry, suspecting that when Biddy disappeared from 16th century Scarborough for a few days she was going to Gladys, had tied the pendant around her neck. It was his way of telling Uncle Norman that he was alive. He had hoped he would understand the message.

"Gladys!" Norman said later. "Wherever Biddy is going for days on end is where I believe Henry is too!"

Norman told the police and they followed Biddy here and there, but of course it all came to nothing.

Chapter 16

Unravelling Mysteries

H e n r y looked at Tom. His head trying to make sense of it all... "But that can't be right," he said. "I've got grandparents...or at least, I did have, they died...but...I know Mum was adopted...but still...and how can you be my grandfather when you're from another century?"

"I can only imagine," said Tom, "that someone found my little girl wandering around in Cambridge, your time, and took care of her. I believe she told me she had been adopted. But she's my daughter and I'm so glad to have her back with me." He blew his nose into a handkerchief.

Henry's head was spinning with questions... "How did she get into my time?" he asked. "Through a painting?"

"She did," said Tom. "We were at the Scarborough fair together and someone was selling paintings. She was next to me, looking at a picture of Cambridge and the next thing I knew she had disappeared. I wouldn't have believed it unless I had seen it with my own two eyes. And the real give away was a small girl and a white cat suddenly appearing in the corner of the picture."

"Oh yes," said Henry, remembering Christmas Day at Gladys's house when Biddy had appeared in that painting. Then he said, "How could a picture of Cambridge in my time be in a fair in the 1500s? That doesn't make sense!"

"I know," said Tom. "I'm not sure myself but Biddy was with us...Biddy does belong to Gladys, as much as she belongs to anyone...and there was a picture of Cambridge in 16th Century on the stall. I began to believe that none of us could go through without Biddy. There was talk of my great uncle travelling and, you know, he had a white cat too. So, I began wondering if..."

"...if it was Biddy!!" Henry finished Tom's sentence for him and looked up at the old man in wonder. Tom nodded.

"Anyway, the picture at the fair was a picture of a college...Peterhouse, if you know it... that still looks just the same today," said Tom. (Henry remembered that Cambridge was very old.) "Somehow, with Biddy, Rosie travelled forward in time to Gladys living in Highcroft Road. That's what I think. Most confusing. And mysterious. But there's more things in heaven and earth than you or I know Henry. And Biddy is a very mysterious cat."

Henry nodded. "She certainly is!" He said.

"So how did you...how had you got to Cambridge that time I saw you at the Christmas market?"

"Well, I had bought that picture of Cambridge from the fair and took a chance and tried going with Biddy one time. My goodness, it was frightening at first! But you know all about that! When the room started whirling ...Ugh!" Henry nodded earnestly in agreement. "I had been doing it for many years by the time I met you at the market," he said. "But I could never find my Rosie. I didn't really know where to look, you see. But she came back to me." (Here his eyes became watery remembering and his voice caught.) "I found her wandering by the castle...the picture now in the room where you came through had been in a different room then...downstairs somewhere and she was able to slip out. She realised she was in another time quite quickly and somehow got hold of some clothes...as you did...you're both quick witted..." he said proudly. "Anyway. I found her wandering and I knew her straight away. I wanted to help her and she seemed to be able to trust me quite quickly. Of course, she had completely forgotten who I was," (That crack in his voice came again.) "She only remembered everything from your time...including you Henry...and she was very distressed and worried about you. It was then I realised I would have to find a way to send her back...because of you. I didn't want a child to grow up without a mother as she had. Even though I wanted to keep her here."

93

"Is the picture the one in my bedroom here?" asked Henry.

"Yes, that's the one," said Tom

"Why don't we just go through that one now?"

"Because it doesn't work that way at first. For some time, I could only go back and forth between two pictures. Then one day I found I was able to travel through any painting I wanted, but you won't be able to yet. You will have to use the first one two you went through. My theory is that it is a loop hole in time...or a wormhole, I've heard it called. A link between the two worlds. You might call it a portal. When I go with Biddy using the painting I bought, we arrived with quite a bang in front of Kings College. Luckily the painting was quite unusual...painted from the view of a small cobbled lane opposite and we would arrive there. We sometimes gave people quite a shock...but no one ever questioned us."

"When I wanted to go back I went to a book shop in St. Edwards's passage and found a book about the history of Scarborough with a painting from my time in it. I wasn't sure if it would work, but I took it into a privy in a cafe and tried."

"What's a privy?" asked Henry.

"It's what you call a toilet!" said Tom.

"Ohh!" said Henry.

"Anyway, I found the painting in the book worked! I bought that book to be sure I could always return."

"So," said Henry carefully, slowly, hardly daring to believe the possibilities. "We could go through any other painting...I mean to a different place not Cambridge...any at all, as long as Biddy was with us?"

"As far as I know, yes."

"Wow," said Henry.

Henry's head was spinning and he felt a bit light headed. He was quiet for a bit. "Why did you come to Cambridge at Christmas he said?"

"Do you know?" said Tom. "I just like going there! It's so interesting and wonderful to be able to time travel. Of course, I was always hoping I might see you...and I did! I recognised you immediately...you looked just like your Mother...plus Biddy seemed to know you too."

"Why didn't you just send Mum back with Biddy before now?" said Henry

"I tried of course...but it wouldn't work Henry. I could never think of a way to get back into the castle ...you can see...it isn't easy to get in there. This party is quite the opportunity!"

Henry was quiet again ...then... "What about you?" he said. "You're our family too, Tom...maybe we could stay with you..."

Tom looked down sadly and shook his head.

"Henry as much as I would love that, things would never be quite right. Your Mum would never know you as her son...and what about your Uncle Norman? Wouldn't you like to see him again?"

Henry thought of Uncle Norman, wondering where Henry was and tears began to form in his eyes.

"Yes...I'm worried about him...I think about him a lot," he said. "I miss him...and he doesn't have any other family close by."

"Henry wherever you are, your Mum will never know me as her Father. That's sad for me but true. She was too little, when she first left me, to remember me. At least if you went home she would remember you again, at least that's what I'm hoping and I could come and visit...and somehow...become part of your lives in some way."

"Wouldn't I forget you?" said Henry

"I'm not sure, but I don't think so Henry," said Tom. "You see you haven't forgotten your home or even begun to yet! Your Mum had certainly begun to forget by the time two weeks had gone past...that is how long you have been here. You are as clear as the day you arrived. I believe you may be more like me Henry...able to time travel without forgetting. But for now, we just want to get you home somehow. Put poor Uncle Norman's mind at rest. Get your Mum back."

"But won't she be confused when she goes home?"

"At first, maybe. But I am hoping as the days go by she will remember her life in Cambridge. I believe it's the best for everyone."

He looked down at Henry and ruffled his hair... "You know..." he said, "I used to have red hair just like yours!"

Tom looked at Henry and put one arm around him. "I'm so glad I've found you!"

"Me too," said Henry, feeling happy. They sat together for a while then Tom said, "Time for supper!" and they got up and headed back into the cottage.

Chapter 17

Brother Jok

J o k had been watching his brother for a long time. He had watched with amazement when Tom started being seen with a beautiful woman who looked so much like Beatrice. Young enough to be his daughter...maybe she was her...but if she was, she had no idea and had lost her memory, folks said. He had confronted Tom soon after she first came back... "Who is the girl? Why is she staying with you?" His brother had said he had found her wandering, lost by the castle and that he had rescued her and taken her home. The world wasn't kind to penniless women wandering alone he had said. He said he had chosen to be her protector.

"So, do you intend to make a wife of her for yourself?" said Jok. "No indeed not," Tom had replied. "I am just as I say...her protector." Jok didn't buy it. He didn't know what was going on...but something was...and now...this boy...where had he come from? After seeing them together at the tailors he had wanted to know more.

He decided to pay a visit to his brother's house, although he hadn't done so for nearly two years. "After all," he said to himself. "Can't a man visit his own brother?" He would see what he could discover.

He set off one evening to Tom's place. He knew they would be cautious of him, but he knew his brother had a big heart and would receive him, desiring reconciliation. He would approach the house carefully...he might overhear something that would be useful...something that would explain things a bit more.

As he approached the little cottage he saw Tom and that boy sitting on a pile of logs talking. It seemed an intense discussion. He stealthily crept around until he was near enough to catch their words and what he heard amazed him. He stayed until Tom and Henry had gone in. He didn't need to visit now. He had heard all the answers he needed and more. He crept quietly away, trying to absorb what he had learnt. "So - Tom is a Voyager!" he said to himself. He had heard of such things. There was always hushed talk in his family about a Great - Great Uncle who, it was said, could come and go and he pleased through time...a 'Voyager'. It was very mysterious and no one had all the facts, but it had intrigued Jok from being a young boy. Most of the family didn't believe it...he hadn't really but he had wished it was true. And to think his brother had time travelled! He felt consumed with jealously. From a young age, he had always felt that Tom was the favoured one in the family, as well as having married the girl he had loved himself. He had no real reason to hate his brother...Tom had done nothing to him. Yet he had let bitterness and jealously consume his heart and it had grown in him like a poisonous weed. It was so large in him now that it completely covered him. It was the first thing people encountered when they met him. And unawares of why, they rejected him almost straight away. Which added to his loneliness. Yes, he was a lonely, bitter man who hated one other more than anything and blamed him for all his misfortunes...

"Why...all I need is that cat!" he said out loud. And began plotting to kidnap Biddy from that time on.

Chapter 18

The Day of the Party

I t was the morning of the party and Rosie was very
excited. She never been to a party...at least...she didn't
think she had. Tom and Henry were more apprehensive
as they realised that this was possibly the only time
they would be able to try to get back to the picture of
Cambridge that was hanging in Ben's bedroom. Tom
and Henry knew they would have to take Biddy along
too or going home wouldn't work. "How to smuggle a
cat into a party held at the castle...not easy," said Tom.
Biddy was very much her own cat as we've said before.
She wasn't accustomed to doing as she was told. But
eventually they settled on putting her inside Toms coat
and hoping for the best. He would refuse to take it off if
asked.

Rosie had made herself a dress which she looked
very beautiful in. She had also made clothes for Henry.
He looked very smart, wearing the style of 1580,
although not as fancy as the noblemen in the castle
would be, but then no one expected him to be, as this
was a party for all the villagers and some of them
would have no new clothes at all.

Tom had decided to wear his old 'good' clothes as there was more room for a little white cat of average size under there. No one would expect an eccentric old man who played the flute at the market to be dressed smartly.

Underneath his clothes Henry was wearing the 21st century ones he had arrived in. He was hopeful he would be leaving for good.

They made their way to the fair...they had decided to spend the day there first and then go on to the castle in the evening.

Tom had brought his whistle and this time, Rosie had agreed to sing. Henry remembered her going to folk clubs back in Cambridge, loving the old English tunes. She had always said, "I don't know why really... but they make me feel...safe...at home." Henry realised now that she would have had a memory of them from when she was three years old with her father.

He took a moment to look around the fair. "Wow!" He said to himself. "Can all this be real?" He was in the middle of a fair in 1580! He wanted to soak in each sight and sound. There was music coming from different places, the smell of food cooking, and the cries of merchants selling goods. This was wonderful. No one back home would believe him. If he ever got home that is. And if he did...he knew he wouldn't be able to come back and forth, as the picture to get back to Cambridge was in Ben's room and that was always going to be tricky. So, this might be the last time he visited 16th century England and he wanted to enjoy the experience.

Meanwhile Jok, who had been watching for an opportunity to take Biddy was following them from a distance. He couldn't seem to get a chance whilst at the fair. He had thought it would be the ideal time. Biddy was sitting very near Tom as he played, making money for the day from all the tourists. She really helped to catch people's attention ...they would bend to stroke her and the put money in the hat. Rosie's singing was lovely too and she and Tom were in their element. However, try as Jok might he could never see an opportunity to take Biddy. He skulked around all day, trying to look nonchalant. Tom saw him once or twice but Jok took care to be out of eyesight as much as possible.

As the day wore on he realised this was not going to be his chance. He thought he'd have to try another day. "After all," he said to himself. "I've waited this long...what's another day or two?"

Jok was also looking forward to the party. He had a small band of acquaintances that he was going with ...they tended to be those who were the trouble makers in the village. They couldn't wait to see inside the castle and be treated so well.

The time for the party began and the villagers started to make their way up to the castle. The way in was lit with flaming torches stuck into the ground.

Henry could hear music coming from inside...it sounded very much like the music Mum had sung or listened to back in England. They were songs with different people singing part harmonies with lots of, "Fa la la's" in them. He felt like he was in a film and once again it took his breath away.

They went in and were shown into the great hall of the castle, lit with more torches. The music changed and there a band of musicians playing different instruments that he had never seen before.

In the great hall was a huge roaring fire and on both sides tables for feasting were placed. They circled right around the great hall - there was room for all the villagers to sit. Those with most influence in the village were seated nearest to Sir Rupert and everyone else was told to sit wherever they liked. Tom was holding a surprisingly relaxed Biddy inside his coat. He did look rather chubbier than he really was but not so you would notice. She was rather a small cat even fully grown. Biddy had fallen asleep and so Tom felt he could eat and enjoy himself as much as he could. The food that came out was brought by servants and was wonderful. Sir Rupert had been generous with his guests. However, Tom noticed that most of the villagers had been served on wooden plates such as they would have had at home, rather than the more valuable ones Sir Rupert and his more important guests were using. "Keeping us in our place!" muttered Tom to himself. "Welcome to supper…but just in case you steal the crockery, have a wooden plate…charming."

Jok and his friends were being rather rowdy as the evening wore on and Rupert surveyed the room wishing he had not had to invite such people. His eyes rested one by one on the women there. "Quite pretty, I suppose," he said to himself of one and another, but as he saw Henry, Tom and Rosie sitting together he let out his breath in a gasp. Rosie looked beautiful. Her strawberry blond hair was catching the light with its red highlights. Her cheeks were flushed with good wine and food and she just looked…well, lovely.

Rupert at that moment thought she was the loveliest woman he had ever seen. "I must dance with her," he said. "But I won't make it obvious…I'll dance with others first." He had a quiet word with a servant who hurried off to get the evening's entertainment in progress.

A jester entered the room and told some jokes, turned a few somersaults and cartwheeled out of the room. Everyone was laughing and clapping. The louder members of the gathering were rowdy in the corner. Rupert kept an eye on them.

And an eye on Rosie too.

Then came some other entertainment, juggling and storytelling and then…a dance called a Branle which Rupert had chosen, as nobility and ordinary people alike knew it.

105

He danced with a couple of other girls and finally came to Rosie...

He held out his hand to her and said, "May I have the pleasure of this dance?"

Rosie was a bit unsure but took his hand hesitantly and got up to join him. Tom watched keenly as they danced together. He soon saw that Rupert liked her very much indeed and that worried him. He was still thinking about the boy in the tower and what that said about the kind of person Sir Rupert might be. What worried him more was Rosie's cheeks were starting to flush as he talked to her and her eyes were sparkling. Still it was only a dance...he was dancing with different ones and she was his latest choice that was all. He turned his attention back to how to get Henry, Biddy *and* Rosie upstairs at the right time. He decided to try when the next dance began and checked to see if Biddy was alright. There she was under his coat, but starting to wake. As the dance ended he said to Henry, "Ok, let's try for it now." Henry nodded and they both waited for Rosie to come back to them. She had a good colour in her cheeks and was smiling. "What a nice man!" she said, looking back over her shoulder at him, looking at her.

"I'm glad Rosie. Henry and I were thinking of going for a walk...would you like to come?"

"A walk?" said Rosie. "Where to?" Not really wanting to leave at all.

"Just a little look around...I'm sure Sir Rupert won't mind if we explore a little bit."

"I'm sure he will," said Rosie looking at the guards around the doors. "He may be throwing a party for us, but he probably still doesn't want us traipsing all over his castle Tom...what are you thinking?"

Tom looked at Rosie and at Henry. This was a problem he had anticipated. He decided to appeal to Rosie's curiosity. "There's something I've found out about and I very much want to see it," he said.

"What is it?" said Rosie, her interest piqued.

"I'll show you when we get there Rosie. Come on love, don't you trust me?"

"I do…" said Rosie. "But...alright then." She did trust Tom very much and knew this must be worth seeing or doing or he wouldn't have said so.

Tom watched the guards...they were interested in the dancing and were watching some of the village girls who were giggling on a table near where they were standing. The guards were laughing and nudging one another. They were standing in front of an archway covered with a curtain and Tom said... "Go on Henry...see if you can get through there...I'll follow. And then Rosie last." Rupert still had his eye very much on Rosie which was an irritant to Tom as he realised this could jeopardise things. Henry and Tom inched their way around the wall very slowly stopping to chat with this one and that one as if merely making the rounds. Eventually he was very near to the curtain which covered the way out. The guards were still chatting and laughing and didn't notice him slip through. Tom was able to follow fairly easily. Even Rosie was able to slip out after them as Rupert was talking briefly to another girl and had taken his eyes off her.

They slipped out and found their way through the castle as best they could. They decided to say they were lost if anyone found them. But most of the staff were at the party tonight so the castle was emptier than usual. It was all hands on deck for such a big affair and obviously one that was so important to Rupert.

They found it quite easy to get to where they thought the tower should be and found it unguarded. Indeed, Ben had been locked in for the evening with no one to guard the door. (Tom was good at picking locks so this possibility didn't worry him and he was prepared.)

Rosie said, slightly impatiently, "Now Tom, what is it you wanted to show me?" She had rather been enjoying herself dancing with Rupert and wanted to get back.

"Just a minute Mu...Rosie," said Henry. "You'll see." They climbed the stairs towards Ben's room.

Henry's heart was hammering with excitement...and nerves...he realised all at once they could be caught or they could be going home...it seemed like it was really going to be happening...and he was taking Mum with him!

108

Tom put his foot on the old windy staircase. Henry remembered climbing up stair cases like this on school trips. They had always made him dizzy.

They were making their way upwards when...it happened...Biddy jumped out of Toms coat and ran down the stairs.

"Biddy?" said Rosie. "What in the world is she doing in your coat?"

"Biddy!" whispered Tom urgently.

At about the same time...or it seemed like it, they heard another voice.

"Jok!!" said Rosie in surprise.

"Well then Biddy, come to Jok," they heard a voice say. A voice full of longing and excitement, but trying to sound calm...they all went backwards down the stairs and saw Jok grab Biddy and stuff her in his jacket.

"Jok!!" said Tom, urgently, as quietly as he could. "Put her down at once."

"Who do you think you are, ordering me around?" said Jok. "I know what this cat can do and now it's my turn to have some fun."

"What is he talking about?" said Rosie.

Tom shook his head at Rosie as if to say, 'Never mind.'

"I wondered what you were up to when I saw you sneaking off. What were you doing?" he said.

"Exploring the castle," said Henry a bit weakly and unconvincingly.

"Exploring the castle?" said Jok, mockingly. "I don't think so...something's going on."

"Where did you even come from little boy...what? Suddenly Tom's got a son?"

"How about you lady...who are you really?"

Rosie looked distressed and confused. She looked at Tom.

"What is going on Tom? Why did you bring us out here?"

As Tom was struggling to know what to say and wondering what on earth to do they heard another sound. Footsteps. Jok, quick as a flash, ran down another corridor and disappeared holding Biddy tightly.

Chapter 19

Jok Goes Travelling

J o k ran as fast as he could and found a way out of the
castle. He had done it! He had the cat. He felt
triumphant!

Biddy, surprisingly, was not scratching or fighting
to get away but allowed herself to be carried.

"I was meant to have this cat," he said to himself.
"I should have always been the one..."

Biddy inside his coat calmly licked her paw.

Jok ran out and away from the castle, running until
he thought there was no more need...then he settled to
an easier pace, making his way through the woods
towards his home in the village.

Jok hadn't always been a jealous, angry person like
he was today. As a child, he had been very kind and
loving by nature, but he was not his parents favourite;
Tom was and Jok knew it. Hurt and sadness grew to let
in bitterness and self-pity, jealousy, envy and rage. This
is how he was today. Not towards all his friends but
really just towards Tom. However, Tom was well liked
in the village and people didn't want to hear Jok
running him down...so they isolated him further. He
still had some old friends from when he was

younger...ones that remembered him before he became so unhappy and bitter. Tom knew this and felt so sad for him but pride always stopped Jok from receiving kindness and love from his brother.

When he got to his small stone cottage he went inside quickly. Inside he had a picture he had bought in preparation for this day. A picture of a beautiful home such as only a rich yeoman or nobleman could afford. His idea was that he would go through the picture and make it his home. He was very excited indeed. He sat prepared before the picture and held Biddy nervously. Biddy looked peacefully at him and blinked. He closed his eyes and waited. Nothing happened. "What am I supposed to do here?" he said to Biddy, shaking her a bit. "Say something special? Do something different? What should I...?"

Just then the room stared spinning before him just as it had for Henry and Tom at different times and Jok found himself experiencing the same spinning sensation, while his feet were quite still. Colours and impressions spun around him...his little stone cottage walls of grey blurred together and slowly, gradually the colours changed and he found himself suddenly standing in a room he didn't recognise. Before he had time to look around the door of the room opened and the master of the house entered.

Jok spun around and the man shouted, "Thief! Vagabond! Trespasser! What do you mean by coming into my home uninvited?" With one or two large steps, he was upon Jok and had him pinned to the ground whereupon he put his foot on him and shouted, "Agnes Agnes!" A small nervous looking servant woman rushed into the room

"Fetch the constable Agnes!" he shouted. "I have a criminal here!"

Agnes scurried off to do as she was told.

The house belonged to a man who had had the painting of his home done professionally which had been stolen by an unscrupulous fellow called Jeremiah Flack and found its way to a market stall where Jok had bought it. He had done a good deal for Jok who was an acquaintance of his.

Jok looked wildly around for Biddy but couldn't see her anywhere.

"Please sir," he said. "I'm not a thief sir!"

"Not a thief?" said the man. "Then what, pray are you? And why are you in my house?"

Jok could think of no answer but the truth.

"I …I…I…came through a picture," he stammered. "With my cat…" his voice trailed off.

"Oh!" said the man, lowering his voice slightly. "Maybe not a thief but certainly a madman indeed."

The man, whose name was John, was not an unkind man and began to wonder if this was a poor insane creature who had wandered into his home. Still very firmly with his foot on him he said, "Well, you may be mad but you will still be tried by the law and this may help your cause, but you can't be allowed to just wander into people's homes and frighten them like that."

Sure enough, in time, the constable came and took him away.

Jok, fully realising the punishment for thieving was hanging, made the most of being thought mad and pretended to be so whilst he was put in a cell until sentence. He was very frightened and regretted like anything stealing Biddy who was nowhere to be seen and now he was stuck in this damp cell with possibly a mad house to look forward to. He wondered if Tom would be able to help him. And here we must leave him to his own thoughts.

Chapter 20

Sir Rupert's Hospitality

M e a n w h i l e Tom, Henry and Rosie stood stock still and tried to hide... "Quickly!" said Tom... "Up the staircase!" Quietly they went further up again. They waited as the guards went passed...Jok had told them off about his brother wandering about...he was friends with one of the guards. He had said to his friend.

"Let me go and find them first and then follow in about ten minutes."

So, sure enough, here they came.

They seemed, at first, to have got away with it but then a guard came back and thought he would check the staircase and found all three. "What do you think you're up too? You're all coming with me." He escorted them, non-too gently, down to the cells. "You can wait here till Sir Rupert hears about this," he said.

Henry and Tom looked at each other. Tom knew better than Henry what sort of punishment could follow crime like this. So, he tried to smile reassuringly at him. "Oh Tom!!" said Rosie. "What are we going to do now!"

"It smells down here!" said Henry, holding his nose. It was a horrible mix of damp and something else he couldn't quite put his finger on. But Tom knew... "Rats!" he said, and then wished he hadn't as Rosie looked horrified.

Just then, a raggedy looking black shadow ran past the cell causing Rosie to screech out in horror!

Meanwhile it had not escaped Sir Rupert's attention that his favourite lady had gone from the great hall and when the guards came and told him three villagers had been found wandering around the castle...he wondered if one of them was Rosie. He excused himself from the proceedings, which were going on well without him and made his way down to the cells with the guard. There was a nasty smell coming from the dungeons and he wondered if there were rats down there. They really didn't use these cells anymore, but they came in useful sometimes.

Sure enough, when he got to the cell he saw Rosie and the two companions she'd had at dinner. He decided to be kind, as he was still keen to get to know Rosie better.

"Good evening friends. Can I ask what you were doing leaving the party at such a jolly time?

"We wanted to explore the castle!" said Henry. "We've only ever seen it from outside before," Tom said.

"It's very grand," added Rosie. She was furious with Tom for this turn of events.

116

Sir Rupert was a little suspicious of them. He had heard they were halfway up the stairway to the boy's tower...no he couldn't take any chances...but neither did he want to scare Rosie off either.

"And who are these people Rosie?" he said smiling in a kinder way than he felt.

"This is Tom, who took me in after my parents died and looked after me like a father. And this is Henry...another orphan," she said. She realised she was stretching the truth, but then she didn't really know what the truth was herself, not fully.

"I see," said Sir Rupert. "How kind you are sir." If there was a trace of sarcasm in his voice it was barely there.

He looked at Rosie. She really was beautiful. And she had danced so well. More like a lady than a seamstress from the village. But what had they been doing sneaking around the castle? Were they innocently exploring or did they know something? He thought of the saying, 'Keep your friends close and your enemies closer.' Since he wasn't yet sure which they were he came up with a scheme.

"Seeing as you are so interested in my home," he said. "I want to invite you to stay as my special guests for the night. You will have the best rooms and be treated like royalty. I insist!" he said, seeing that Tom looked uncertain. "It's the least I can do after my guards here locked you up in our cells! Come, forgive us and let me make amends!"

117

Tom, Henry and Rosie had very different reactions to this. Tom was thinking, 'I don't really trust this man...and I don't like the way he's been looking at Rosie. I know he's not married...maybe that's what all this is about. On the other hand, we would be in the castle itself! What better way to get a chance to get them home! I know Biddy will make her way back to us on time.'

Henry thought, 'Wow! Brilliant to be a guest in a castle!'

And Rosie was thinking, 'This is wonderful!! And how handsome Lord Rupert is! He really seems to like me.'

"Thank you, sir!" said Tom. "Would you like that Rosie and Henry?"

"Oh yes!" cried Henry.

"Yes," said Rosie, blushing and looking down as Rupert looked keenly at her.

"Then it is settled!" said Rupert. "Now shall we re-join the party? Unlock these poor people!" he told his guards, scolding them as if they themselves were entirely to blame.

They went back to the room where the people were still making merry and a lot of them had had a good deal too much to drink. They enjoyed the rest of the evening. No one had really noticed they were gone.

The evening ended and the villagers made their way home through the dark night...all excited and happy at having had such a wonderful time. "Well, old

Rupert's not so bad after all!" One man was heard to say on his way out. "What a gentleman he is!" said another.

Rosie, Tom and Henry were shown to their rooms and what rooms!! Four poster beds just as sumptuous as those in Ben's room, with beautiful drapes and tapestry on the walls. They settled down for the night, each one thinking his or her own thoughts.

'I hope Biddy comes back soon,' thought Tom. 'I'm pretty sure she could make it through the window of my room.'

'This is amazing!' thought Henry. 'We didn't get in trouble and now we're in the castle for longer...but oh dear! What about Biddy? We can't do anything without her!'

'What beautiful rooms!' thought Rosie. 'Why I feel like quite the lady here.'

And so, we will leave them to sleep in their grand beds and join them tomorrow.

Chapter 21

Rescue Plan

I t has been some time since we talked of Ben...the poor lonely child in the tower. He had heard the voices coming up the stairs towards his room and had hoped against hope that they were coming to see him. He wasn't sure but he thought he recognised one of the voices as being Henry's. 'He's come back to see me!' he thought. 'Just as he promised to!' But then they seemed to get quieter again and he heard other voices he didn't recognise. He pressed his ear to the door in and attempt to catch what was being said but to no avail.

Ben's welfare was being discussed meanwhile between the two people who knew him best and who had been sworn to secrecy. Thomasina and Mr. Baggott were both paid a good wage to keep their mouths shut about Ben. Both were good people at heart and after struggling with their consciences in their jobs, they had begun meeting. It was good to talk about the child who worried them both so and whom they had grown so fond of. Not only that but they were also starting to feel fond of each other too. So, they began to meet often and it was such a time, as they were walking in the forest, that they both agreed something had to be done for Ben.

"Thomasina, you must know by now how much I care for you?" said Mr. Baggott, a little awkwardly and blustering a bit.

Thomasina blushed and said, "Yes, I feel the same way."

"Well," he said. "Would you then do me the honour of becoming my wife?"

"Yes!" said Thomasina. "I would!"

"Wonderful!" said Mr. B and they kissed each other and then held hands and walked happily along together for some time.

"Thomasina," said Mr. Baggott. "I have a plan to help Ben...would you like to hear it?" he said, looking all around himself and drawing her deeper into the woods so that they would not be heard.

"Yes!" she said. "You know I want to help that poor child more than anything."

"I have friends here from France who have come for the fair," he said. "They are staying with me presently. I want to marry you as soon as possible and then go to Ben and tell him exactly what his uncle is doing to him and ask him if he wants to come with us to France with our friends. They return at the end of this week so we don't have long. We can raise him as our own boy. Rupert won't come after him as no one knows about him here and he wouldn't want them to.

The boy may yet have a chance of a good life. You and I, Thomasina, we could raise him as our own...and who knows and loves him better than us?"

"Do you really think it would work?" she said

"I don't see why not," said Mr. Baggott.

"What if he doesn't want to come and tells his uncle about our plan?"

"If he doesn't want to come and we suspect he will tell his uncle we will go anyway ourselves. It would be safer. What do you think?"

"It's worth a try. After all, neither of us have family here to leave behind."

Both had lost their parents as quite young people. Thomasina had gone into the castle as a maid when quite young and only really knew that life. She felt it would be an adventure to go to France.

"We'll tell him today after his lessons. Come up to the room as you normally do at one for his lunch and I will still be there. We will need the help of God for this."

"You're right," she said and quietly breathed a prayer.

Later that day they carried out their plan. Thomasina met Mr. Baggott in Ben's room and they approached the subject together. Ben listened and for some reason he just knew they were telling the truth. He agreed to come. "I'm just sad I won't see my friend

Henry again," he said then straight away wished he hadn't.

"Who is your friend Henry?" said Mr. Baggott.

"I met him here in this room!" he said. "He told me he had come through the picture over there."

They all looked at the picture of Cambridge on the wall.

"Really!" said Thomasina and looked at Mr. Baggott who was stroking his beard in a concerned way...

"I think you might have dreamt him Ben," she said.

"I didn't!" said Ben. "He's real! I don't know if he really got in through the picture...he didn't seem mad...but ...he was nice and he was the only friend I've ever had of my own age. I let him out of the window by tying my bed sheets together."

"Now that's an idea," said Mr. Baggott who had been wondering how they were going to get out of the castle and was glad to change the subject. Being locked up his whole life was clearly starting to drive the boy mad with loneliness.

"Why have you never tried to get out that way Ben?"

"Because of the wild and dangerous peasants!" said Ben.

Mr. Baggott had heard him use this term before and asked him now to explain more. The explanation confirmed all their plans to get him out as soon as possible. They began planning at once.

Chapter 22

A Proposal

M e a n w h i l e, Rosie had been having a wonderful time as a guest in the castle. Henry had always liked history, was enjoying himself very much too. He kept thinking, 'This will never happen to me again! I am in a 16th century castle!' However, Tom was not so happy. He didn't like Rupert, didn't trust him...and there was no chance of getting back through the picture until Biddy was there.

Rupert had wined and dined them royally, there could be no argument with that. The food had been wonderful. They had been entertained well. Lord Rupert had taken him out hunting. But he was longing to either get on with the real reason he was here or get home.

Rosie, as I said before was having a wonderful time. Lord Rupert kept paying her special attention and even though most people didn't think he was particularly handsome, Rosie did and all ladies like to be made to feel special. He gave her the best chair at dinner and told her how nice she looked all the time. Tom saw all this and worried more. Henry saw it and he didn't like it either as he knew more about Lord Rupert than his Mum...but both Tom and Henry knew that they had been caught snooping around and that they couldn't object or ask to go home just yet...besides, while they were in the castle, they had a better chance of getting home. So, they spoke together and decided not to say anything to Rosie at the moment.

Rupert was also enjoying himself. He wasn't sure what he was going to do with Tom and Henry when he and Rosie were married...but, for now, they were a means to an end. One thing he was sure about...he wanted to make Rosie his wife.

So, one evening he arranged for Tom and Henry to practice some archery with some of the courtiers and sent a servant to Rosie's room.

Rosie's head shot up at the knock on the door. She had just finished changing after supper.

"Come in," she said.

"My lady, Sir Rupert requests the pleasure of your company in the rose garden," said the servant.

"Oh!" said Rosie. "Thank you."

The servant left and Rosie made her way down to the garden, wondering what he wanted. As she approached the garden she saw Sir Rupert sitting on a bench surrounded by rose bushes.

"There you are Rosie!" he said. "Do come and join me...isn't it a lovely evening?"

And it really was. It was still light and the sun's last rays were brightening the sky. The air was dusky.

Much as Rosie liked being made to feel special, she felt a little nervous to be on her own with Sir Rupert. She wondered where Tom and Henry were.

Sir Rupert produced a rose he had just cut himself from the garden. "A rose for a rose," he said.

"Thank you," she said and took it.

"Rosie, I must tell you," said he. "That since I first saw you I have been most impressed with you. Most impressed indeed."

"Oh really?" said Rosie blushing

"Yes," said Sir Rupert, taking her hands and looking deeply into her eyes. "I have really enjoyed the time we have spent together here."

"Thank you," said Rosie. "So have I."

"And I think you are very beautiful," said Sir Rupert.

"Oh!" said Rosie. "Thank you Sir!" and she blushed again.

"And so, I wondered if you might consider…"

('Is he going to say what I think he is??' thought Rosie)

"…marrying me?" he said.

'Oh, my goodness?' thought Rosie. 'This is a bit fast!'

Out loud she said, "Oh!! Thank you Sir Rupert ...can I please consider it further before replying? I think I would like to but I need time to think."

"Yes Rosie of course. Well, may I pay you court?" Rosie looked slightly surprised then nodded and looked down shyly. Rupert felt impatient. He had hoped his riches compared to her peasant lifestyle would have made the answer easy. This would be a harder fish to catch than he had thought.

'Patience,' he said to himself. 'I can win her round. She hasn't replied yet. I must be patient.'

Rosie had a lot to think of that evening as she sat in her room. How wonderful it was to be wanted like that! She couldn't remember being pursued like this before and yet...something about it felt familiar. As if it had happened before with someone else. Another thing that confused her was that she had thought his question to 'court' her old fashioned...and yet it was quite the custom in 1580 and not old fashioned at all. Her thoughts and feelings were mysterious sometimes and once again she wondered about gaps in her memory and the feeling of only being 'Half-here'. She decided to talk to Tom about it and see what he said. She didn't love Sir Rupert, but then she hardly knew him. 'And to think that if we were married, I would be mistress of this whole castle!' she thought. 'Tom and Henry could live here too!' And yet even as she pondered on it she knew her feelings and thoughts were sometimes muddled and she didn't trust her own judgement. She decided to talk to Tom about it and see what he said.

Chapter 23

Disappearance Discovered

It was four in the morning when a lithe furry form padded its way softly through the courtyard of the castle. She had come through the forest and into the castle whilst the drawbridge was down. She had kept out of sight quietly in the shadows watching the hustle and bustle of castle life throughout the day, sleeping and washing intermittently. Now she was aiming for one place and one place only...

She scaled the wall to Tom's bedroom easily and with a light thud of four velvet feet she arrived there. She jumped on the bed and curled up in the 'v' of his bent knees and went back to sleep. She wasn't in a hurry. She was right on time.

Tom woke as the first rays of sunlight came through the window of his bedroom. He stretched and paused, confused at the soft bundle lying behind his legs. He looked blearily rubbing his eyes, "Biddy?" he said. "You're back!" Biddy woke and purred softly, walking up to Tom and sitting on his chest with her face next to his. He stroked her and laughed, "You're always on time Biddy," he said. "Do you know something I don't old girl? Is it soon?" Biddy purred and lay her head down for another sleep. Tom lay back on the bed encouraged and comforted to have her back. He soon slipped back into sleep as well.

Later after breakfast Rosie said to Tom that she must speak to him alone. Tom agreed and afterwards they both headed for the garden.

"What is it Rosie?" asked Tom.

"Tom...Rupert has asked me...has asked me to marry him!!" she said.

"What!!" said Tom. "My goodness...and what did you say Rosie?"

"Well I told him I would think about it," she said. "Tom...you're my dearest friend in the world...what do you think about this?"

Tom knew exactly what he thought but wasn't sure how to tell her. Then, suddenly he knew what to do.

"Rosie before you make your decision I want to show you something that might help you to decide."

"Really?" said Rosie. "Ok, what is it?"

"I'll show you tonight," said Tom. "Meet me by my room at eleven. But don't breathe a word to anyone about this. Promise me you won't."

"I won't Tom," she said. "I promise."

Rosie felt intrigued by this news and when Rupert pressed her again to give him his answer she said, "I will tomorrow Rupert...please be patient with me."

Rupert, not the most patient of men, wondered why she was taking so long. He was used to having his way all the time.

"Yes, my love," he said hoping to win her with some smooth words. "I can wait forever for you if I have to."

'I certainly won't though,' he said to himself. 'If she doesn't say yes soon, they're out.'

The day wore on. Rupert entertained them as graciously as he could for someone whose patience was wearing thin.

"What's wrong with the girl?" he said to himself "I'm sure if I was a peasant like she is and was asked to be married by one such as me...it wouldn't be such a tough decision. My goodness, I won't put up with this kind of behaviour if we marry. She'll have to do as she is told!"

Rosie meanwhile was thinking. 'Rupert has been very kind to me...but sometimes I don't like the look in his eye...I could be imagining it...its lovely to have someone pay me attention...and someone so grand as he is...if I did marry him, Tom, Henry and I would be quite comfortable for the rest of our lives! I mustn't just think of myself...but will Tom want a life like this? He enjoys wandering and singing with Biddy...on the other hand...maybe he only does that to make a bit of money...'

What was happening to Rosie can happen to lot of women. If a man pays them some attention and is kind and generous...they can start to overlook those things which should not be overlooked. That 'look in his eye' was the thing she should have been taking most notice of. It was cold, selfish arrogance in him that she was seeing.

Just as they were sitting and both thinking in these different ways, there was suddenly a shout coming closer and closer to the room where they were… "Sir Rupert! Sir Rupert! Please sir, come at once...something has happened…come now Sir!"

"What is it?" said Rupert snappily...causing Rosie to see that look in his eye and doubt him again.

The only guard who knew about Ben, bent low and whispered in his ear. Rupert went white and got up quickly. "Please continue to enjoy yourselves," he said. "I have some business I must attend to." And with that he swiftly left the room.

Sir Rupert ran along the passages of the castle until he got to the tower stairs where Ben's room was. He took the steps two at a time and taking his key he opened the door and flung it wide. There in the room was...no one at all. He looked at the bedsheets tied to the bedpost and realised that his nephew had escaped. But where could he have gone? Who did he know? He couldn't have got far. He wasn't worried about the boy really, just his own reputation. What a mystery! He thought a moment. Maybe he didn't need Ben after all. Maybe if Rosie said yes to him he would have a son of his own. And if she didn't he would find someone else. Yes, yes… let the boy be. He will either be eaten alive by wolves or he will find somewhere to stay. Or he could be brought back here. Wait…no... then everyone would know what he had done. What he had been planning to do. To keep him in case he didn't produce an heir of his own and then do away with him if he did. Who would ever have known? Only three people...the one who had alerted him, the tutor and the maid servant. They had sworn on their lives not to tell. And their lives would have indeed have been forfeit if they had...and yet... 'Who else does he know?' he thought to himself. 'Maybe he has gone to them.' He scratched his head wondering, thinking.

"Where are Thomasina and Mr. Baggott?" he asked the guard.

"Neither of them have been here today, Sir," said the servant.

"What?" said Rupert. "Well, go to Thomasina's room, go to Mr. Baggott's house...something is going on...something…I need to know!" Fears of people finding him out as the terrible man he was, filled his thoughts. He didn't care about Ben, whether he was alright or not. He only cared about his reputation.

"I have done both Sir," said the guard. "And they are not there."

Ben lifted his pale face to the breeze and felt it lift his hair. Colour came back into his cheeks. His new 'family' Mr. and Mrs. Baggott stood with him, their hearts flooding with hope. They were on the boat back to France with Ben. No one from Scarborough had seen them get on. They had got clean away. They had done it!

"I'm so glad I taught him French," said Mr. Baggott.

"I'll still have to work on mine!" said Thomasina.

"Mon Cherie!" said Mr. Baggott (which means 'my darling' in English) pulling her close into a hug.

"What does that mean again?" said Thomasina.

The sunset clouds were glowing purple and orange swirls. The sun was on fire. They sailed towards it and became a dot on the horizon and then were gone.

The boat sailed into the sunset and was gone over the horizon. A wonderful new life in France was waiting for them all.

Chapter 24

Remembering Home

R u p e r t said nothing about Ben's disappearance when he returned to be with his guests. One thing was for certain, he would not turn them out just yet...marrying Rosie who seemed quite keen (although currently playing hard to get) was his best chance of getting an heir. And she did have very beautiful hair. And her *eyes*! He shut his own eyes and sighed out loud just thinking of beautiful blue-green pools! He needed to think.

"Please do excuse me again," he said. "I have some business to attend to. I have arranged activities for you all today...please have a wonderful rest of the afternoon and I'll be back for supper." Then he was off. He needed time to think what to do. He took his horse and went riding, the way he liked to think best. He thought he would also keep an eye out for Ben and possibly Thomasina and Mr. Baggott too. No one else knew...no one else could. So off he rode.

Rosie had a pleasant afternoon talking with the ladies in the court. They showed her some embroidery they were doing and she talked of her work as a seamstress. Behind her back, they were asking each other who she was to Rupert and why was she here as a guest. They were pleased to think that he might be thinking of marriage, though confused as to why he would choose such a lowly girl as a match. (The truth is that he felt she would be easier to control than a lady of the court.)

Tom and Henry went out to try archery and enjoyed it...Henry more than Tom whose mind was on the picture and getting them all home.

"Henry," he whispered, whilst it was someone else's turn to shoot an arrow. "Biddy has come back to us! We are going to try for the picture tonight..."

"Oh!" said Henry who was really starting to enjoy himself and wasn't sure now that he ever wanted to go back to Cambridge after all.

"Henry," said Tom. "You are enjoying yourself now but this won't last...you have to go back."

"Why?" said Henry. "I am here with you and Rosie and I'm learning so many wonderful things."

"Henry...the fact that you just called your mother Rosie is one of the reasons! You need to be back where she can remember who you are and you can call her Mum again. And...what about Uncle Norman?" Tom said.

"Oh yes," said Henry and dropped his head. "I had forgotten. We must go back and let him know we are ok."

"You know, Henry...there will doubtless be other doors for you to go through, other adventures for you to go on, but for now you must go back to your time, to 2011."

Tom realised that Henry, whilst he hadn't forgotten his life in 2011, was starting to care less about it and feel more as if he belonged in the 16th century.

Later that night, when all the rest of the household was asleep, Rosie heard a soft knock on her door. She opened the door to find Tom and Henry as she had expected.

Now that Ben was gone Rupert was not worried about them going up those stairs and had positioned his guard elsewhere. Consumed as he was with what had happened to Ben, he did not suspect them being part of the escape, careful as he had been to keep them away from the tower. No, no this was Thomasina and Mr. Baggott's doing. He was furiously angry with them, but clueless as to what they could have done. He knew nothing of Mr. Baggott's French friends and why would he? He was wide awake, seething with rage and confusion. It wasn't Ben he cared about, but he hated to be deceived and made a fool of. He decided to get up and make his way to Ben's room to see if there were any more clues.

Oblivious to this, our friends were making their way along the passageways without a candle. Tom knew the way very well now. He had noted it carefully that first day. They arrived at the stairway and gingerly made their way up.

Rosie wondered what was going on, but didn't ask. She sincerely wanted to find out anything that would help her decide about Rupert. Henry was having a mixture of emotions. He knew that this might be the last trip to Ben's room. He might be leaving the 16th century forever and going home. He might have his Mum back, remembering him again, but he was also going to miss some things. This had been quite an experience. However, the thought of having his Mum back after so long overshadowed everything. He thought too of Uncle Norman and Jonathan and other school friends.

Tom was thinking only of getting this done. He walked quickly, quietly ahead of them, watching and leading the way.

What was Biddy thinking? Who can tell? She lay over Tom's shoulder and washed her right paw. Cool as a cucumber.

They came to the stairs and went up. Softly, one step at a time.

"Where are we?" whispered Rosie.

Tom put a finger to his lips and softly extended his hand to knock on it. But as he did so, it gently creaked open wide. He was surprised, as he had expected it to be locked. It was dark except for the light of a single candle on the mantelpiece.

Tom cautiously stepped in and beckoned the others. Henry stepped in and looked eagerly towards the bed. It was hard to make out Ben's shape...was he there? He stepped towards the bed and looked carefully "Ben...Ben?" he quietly whispered, then rumpled the bedclothes to try to find him.

"Tom!" he cried. "He's not here!"

"No indeed!" said a voice from the corner of the room. "And what I would like to know is, how do you know Ben!"

All eyes turned towards the voice. There just by the light of the candle was Rupert himself. The shadow on the wall behind was long, spiky and menacing in the candle light. When they had first come in he had sidled away into the corner where he would not be seen but now he reappeared. All three felt their hearts began to hammer hard.

"Come, come, don't be shy now!" he said. "What are all three of you doing slinking around my castle in the dark? And how, pray, do you know about my nephew Ben? Does it have anything to do with this?" He held out a letter which he had opened and was reading. It was simply addressed to, *'My friend from the picture.'* It was, of course, for Henry.

Chapter 25

Danger in the Tower

T o m took in the situation at once and tried to take control quickly

"Good evening Sir Rupert," he said, bowing slightly at the waist. "You must forgive us sir, we were in high spirits and merely enjoying a late-night exploration of the castle.

"Oh, I see," said Rupert, laughing contemptuously. "And you expect me to believe that, do you, when I caught you trying to climb up here on the night of the party?" He was white and slightly shaking with rage. "Something is going on and I want to know what. You clearly have met Ben," he said turning abruptly to Henry. "Tell me at once how you know him… or suffer the consequences."

"Who is Ben?" said Rosie innocently. Rupert looked swiftly in her direction. He had forgotten about Rosie. He fully suspected her of being involved in whatever was going on and decided to drop all pretence of being a nice guy.

"Don't play the innocent with me, my dear," he said menacingly, coming a little closer. Tom stepped in front of her. "I feel sure you are involved in all this too. And to think I wanted to marry you! You must know very well who Ben is. Well?" He said turning quickly back to Henry again, who was saying, "Marry her?" to himself

"I repeat the question...how do you know Ben? Answer me!"

Henry went pale and looked at Tom.

Rupert spoke again. "Are you the boy from the picture?" he spat out, thrusting the letter forward into the space between them. Tom again hesitated as he didn't quite know what the letter said.

"May I see that letter?" Tom asked

"I wasn't addressing you...sir!" Rupert replied between gritted teeth.

"May...may I see the letter please?" said Henry. "I think it might be for me."

"Oh, let me read it to you," said Rupert sarcastically.

'Dear Boy from the Picture,

I don't know if you will ever get this. I had hoped you would come back before now to see me... but never mind. As the only friend I have ever had of my own my age, I wanted to say goodbye. I have escaped and I am quite safe. I hope I shall be happy and I hope you are too and that you found who you were looking for.

I doubt I will ever see you again. But if we ever do, it would make me happy.

Your friend,
Ben.'

Henry felt thrilled that he had got away and happy that Ben had been sensible enough to leave out any details, including not using his name.

"Today," said Rupert. "My only nephew and heir Benjamin has run away. I don't know why. I don't know where. And I don't know how he ever met you, but I want to know if you had anything to do with it. It seems likely."

"You don't know why?!" Henry suddenly shouted, forgetting any fear he had had. "You kept him locked up in this room his entire life, never allowing him to meet anyone his own age and only taking him out after dark. Lying to him...I should flipping well want to run away too, anyone would!"

"What on earth is this all about?" said Rosie to Tom. She had decided soon after coming into this scenario that she never wanted to marry Rupert...not ever...not even if he was the last man alive. She was feeling scared and rather disappointed to have seen the other side of this man.

"Quiet!" said Rupert. "I'm warning you...don't whisper to one another or I'll send for the guards."

Tom thought quickly. He didn't think Rupert would be too much for all three of them. He could only shout to the guards if he could get downstairs. Besides it sounded as though all this had been a great secret and he had come here alone at the dead of night...no, he wouldn't be calling anyone.

"I doubt that," said Tom stepping forward. "I don't think you want anyone to know you're here or why. You treated that boy cruelly for his entire life and he's got away. If this got out there would be some repercussions. You know that. No, you're best to keep us in your good books if you know what's good for you."

Rupert was quiet for a moment and then made a move that no one expected. He suddenly grabbed Henry and pulled out a dagger which he put to his throat. Rosie screamed, "Rupert...NO!!" Rosie at this moment was looking startled as well as scared as if the scare had made her remember something very important.

"Quiet!" snapped Rupert. Tom put his arm protectively around her.

"You're a clever one Tom," said Rupert. "But if I've lost one boy another one will do. I intend to keep this one instead and there's nothing you can do about it."

Tom jumped forward. "You will not hurt a single hair on his head!" he shouted.

"What will you do about it old man?" sneered Rupert edging towards the door with Henry. He intended to lock Tom and Rosie in the tower and lock Henry in the dungeons until he had decided what to do.

Tom thought wildly...everything was going wrong...what could he do?

"One minute!" Rupert said. "What did Ben mean 'to the boy in the picture'...tell me!!" he was shaking Henry.

Henry was just wondering what to say when an unexpected turn of events occurred. Suddenly, a streak of white fur was flying through the air and with a feral sound that froze the blood of her friends and terrified her enemy she flew at Rupert's face catching him quite off guard and causing him to cry out in shock. No one expected Biddy to get involved. She had been very quiet hiding under the bed where Rupert couldn't see her. But now, in his shock he dropped the dagger and Tom was quick to pick it up. Henry ran to Tom and Tom pulled both him and Rosie towards the picture of Cambridge that was hanging on the wall. He knew it was now or never. If this went wrong none of them would be going anywhere ever again. All this happened so quickly that by the time Rupert calmed down again Tom, Rosie and Henry were by the picture. Rosie had stopped asking questions and just held on to Tom. Biddy joined them.

"I'll have you all killed!" shouted Rupert seeming to forget his own concern about being quiet. "And I'll skin that cat alive in front of you!" He added, holding his hand resentfully to his face, where Biddy had given him one well justified scratch.

Biddy licked her paw and considered him.

"Maybe so," said Tom. "But it won't be today."

Holding the dagger out towards Rupert to keep him away he softly said.

"Biddy?"

Biddy jumped on Tom's shoulder.

"Goodbye Sir Rupert," said Tom.

All at once a familiar dizzy feeling came over Henry. 'It's happening!' he thought.

He was going home. He felt sad and excited all at once and all in the space of a single second. He found himself remembering in a flash all the faces and experiences he had had whilst here in the 16th century. This all happened like a flash before his eyes, like when people describe their life flashing before their eyes when they think they are going to die.

Rosie was saying, "Tom! Tom! What's happening?" Then shrieking, "Help! Help!"

Tom took her hand as he too felt the spinning feeling and to his great relief the room started to spin around and the colours to blur. The last thing he clearly saw was Rupert standing with an open mouth, amazed. And then he started to see different colours. Colours of brass and yellow, colours of dark wood. They began to turn slower. And slower. And slower. And they stopped. Tom, Biddy, Henry and Rosie were all standing in Gladys's hallway at 3.30pm on a Monday afternoon. In the kitchen, a kettle was whistling on the stove.

They stood stunned for a few seconds until a voice from upstairs rang out.

"Norman? Is that you? The kettle just boiled, would you put water into the teapot? I'll be down in a minute."

With his finger to his lips, urgently motioning to be quiet, especially to a terrified looking Rosie, Tom quietly opened the front door and they all slipped out into the front garden and out through the gate.

Henry looked around him as if seeing it all for the first time. All was just as it always was in Highcroft Avenue. It was quiet and peaceful. The overhead sound of a plane jetting off to somewhere hot, droned above. Rosie jumped and looked scared. There was a cat calmly washing itself on a nearby fence. Biddy ran to join it and was gone. Tom knew he would have to go back soon. He needed to leave them to settle back again to their old lives without him. His heart ached at the thought and he fought back tears.

Rosie looked around her. She felt frightened but at the same time things seemed somehow familiar. Then-like an old-fashioned television, it was as if the fuzzy picture on the screen of her mind was coming into focus. Wait a minute...this...this was Highcroft Avenue where somebody she knew lived...who was it? She looked confused for a moment and then she saw Henry standing in front of her. She stopped, went quite white and said, "Henry?"

"Yes Rosie?" he answered.

"Why are you calling me that?" she replied. "Don't be so cheeky, call me Mum?"

Henry stopped dead in his tracks. Tom too. This was happening much quicker that he had imagined it would. "Mum?" he said, "Oh MUM!!!" and he threw his arms around her and wept for joy. He had waited some long weeks for this and now it was happening.

Rosie held him too and felt tearful, although she wasn't quite sure why. "Henry, I feel as though I have been away for a long time...almost as if I were in a dream," she said.

"You have been Mum," he said, hardly able to believe he could call her that again. "I'll try to explain it to you one day, if I can - but for now, we need to go and see..."

"Uncle Norman!" they both said together as she remembered.

A lithe white shape slipped suddenly into view and jumped up into Tom's arms. "Biddy, old girl!" he said, as she purred in his arms. "Thank you, what a job well done," he whispered into the white fur.

"Well Henry, Rosie, I think the time has come for me to go...for now," said Tom.

Henry threw his arms around him and said, "I don't want you to go! Will we ever see you again?"

"Oh yes," said Tom. "I'll be back. Do you think I'll be able to stay away now that I've met you? Look for me in the market square on the last Saturday of each month. I'll try to be there with Biddy, playing for you." Henry felt a lump in his throat and swallowed hard. "Thank you for everything Grandpa," he whispered into Tom's ear. Tom hugged him tighter and said, "I'm going to miss you so much Henry."

Rosie looked at him strangely. She was still adjusting to being back and was feeling disorientated. She had forgotten who he was... and yet… "Do I know you?" she asked.

Tom looked down to gather his emotions and felt as though his heart would break before looking up again at her. "Yes Rosie - we've met before," he said. He took both her hands and looked into her bluey-green eyes, taking in everything about her. The shape of her eyebrows, so like his own, the coppery tones in her hair, so like her mothers, the confusion and sadness on her face. "I play music in the market square sometimes."

"But I feel as though I know you quite well," she said, searching his eyes in turn. "How very strange!"

"Indeed," said Tom turning away so that she couldn't see his eyes filled with tears.

"Tom is my good friend Mum," said Henry... "I'll tell you all about him soon." Rosie put an arm around Henry and pulled him into her side.

"Goodbye my dears," said Tom. "I'll see you again soon." And after one last long hug with Henry, he walked off down the long street in the direction of the town centre, the old man and the white cat, getting smaller and smaller until they turned the corner and were gone from sight.

So here we leave Rosie and Henry to settle back to their old lives together. As we look back we can see a man coming out of number 16 Highcroft Ave and seeing them come towards him, stumbling backwards in shock... then running forwards with joy, his hat flying off his head behind him as he embraces them to himself.

And as for Tom...well he went back to his cottage in the woods and learnt to play the fiddle, (which made him more money when busking).

Rupert never bothered him as he kept a low profile and kept out of his way. Anyway, Tom found himself travelling more and more often to be with Rosie and Henry. In addition to this, following the incident in the castle tower, everyone was saying that Rupert had gone a bit strange, always talking about savage cats, people disappearing into pictures and laughing almost hysterically at nothing. He had gone into what can only be called a permanent state of shock. Other noblemen from nearby helped to run the estate as best they could.

Ben led a happy and carefree life in France with his new family Mr. Baggott and Thomasina and learned to speak French extremely well...but he never forgot his friend Henry.

As for Jok... Biddy eventually led Tom through the picture in Jok's house to rescue him...and he was a much nicer man and brother after that.

Henry was never sure how to explain to people where he had been. He and Tom had discussed together before he went back, what he was going to say. He decided he would tell people that it was a bit vague to him and that he had been taken somewhere against his will (which was true...he never asked to be whisked into another time). He was deliberately vague about the details and since he was home again and seemed fine, the questions stopped in the end.

Tom could nearly always be found on the last Saturday of each month in the market square and Henry would meet him there, sometimes with Rosie too who had accepted him as Henry's eccentric friend and had liked him immediately herself. They often went out for Chelsea buns and tea after he had played his fiddle in the market place (he loved to treat them from his earnings and would never take no for an answer). However, she never remembered her years in Tom's time, and it was generally assumed that she had had a case of amnesia...something she believed herself.

But nobody except Henry knew why she would sometimes sit and sew clothes that looked as though they belonged to another time...and while she sewed she would always sing:

"Are you going to Scarborough Fair...parsley sage Rosemary and Thyme? Remember me to one who lives there. He once was a true love of mine..."

THE END

Made in the USA
Columbia, SC
26 June 2017